The Marriage Agreement

Margaret MacWilliams

A DELL BOOK

Published by
Dell Publishing Co., Inc.
1 Dag Hammarskjold Plaza
New York, New York 10017

Dell ® TM 681510, Dell Publishing Co., Inc.

ISBN: 0-440-14934-7

Printed in the United States of America
First printing—August 1980

A

CANDLELIGHT EDWARDIAN SPECIAL

CANDLELIGHT REGENCIES

The
Marriage
Agreement

CHAPTER ONE

It was close to eleven o'clock on a March night in the year 1902, and the Duke of Atherton had spent the evening at the Fifth Avenue mansion of Samuel Templeton puzzling over why he had been invited.

A shrewd judge of men, he was well aware that his host rarely made a move without careful calculation, and he suspected that the motive in this instance was an attempt to acquire one of the priceless paintings that hung in the gallery of his ancestral home in Essex.

Settled by the fire in the library, sampling a snifter of superb brandy, he lit a cigar and sensed that the moment of revelation was imminent. With the exception of the food and the wine, both of which had been excellent, he considered the evening had otherwise been abominable. He had always wholeheartedly detested the *nouveau riche*, whether British or American, and Templeton had succeeded in reinforcing his contempt by spending the better part of the last few hours discussing his possessions. He, the Duke, had been forced to admire the marble fireplace in the drawing room, which had once rested in a doge's palace in Venice, the Grand Staircase of Caen marble in the Tudor hallway, the wainscoting of carved French walnut in the library wrested from a chateau in Normandy, his vast collection of paintings from Rembrandt to Renoir and, of course, last but not least, a large collection of photographs of his magnificent yacht, *The Conqueror*.

His host cleared his throat, summoning his attention. "I have a proposition to make," he began and the Duke threw him a glance of ill-concealed distaste.

"I rather suspected you had," Atherton replied dryly. "But I must warn you beforehand that none of my paintings are for sale."

Samuel Templeton rose from his deep wing chair and, turning his back to the fire, stared down at his guest. Somewhere in his middle sixties, tall and massively built, Templeton was the personification of a captain of industry with his thick mane of snow-white hair and his strong craggy features—

the prominent hawklike nose, the full lips half hidden by a bristling moustache, the heavy brows, and above all the eyes, hooded and inscrutable.

"I am not interested in your paintings." Templeton reached for the decanter of brandy and replenished his guest's glass. "I know they're not for sale, but to put it bluntly I thought perhaps you might be."

Astonished, the Duke found himself momentarily speechless. "Are you mad, man?" he finally sputtered.

Samuel Templeton smiled briefly. "I've been called that before and perhaps there is a bit of madness in me, but first hear me out and then make your decision." He crossed to his chair, sinking into it slowly. "For some time you've interested me greatly, both you and your son, so I found it a most happy coincidence to learn you were lecturing here in America. You return to England tomorrow?"

"Yes, on the *Etruria*. But get on with it, Templeton. I'm intrigued to discover why you should think I might be for sale. I thought the day of the indentured servant in your country was long since over."

Samuel Templeton laughed. "It is indeed, but to get to the point quickly, Sir, I know to the last shilling the amount of your debts—that your estate in Essex, for instance, is not only heavily mortgaged but badly in need of repair, and that the same is true of your house in London and your shooting lodge in Scotland."

The Duke of Atherton scowled, shifting uneasily in his chair. "And I'd like to know what bloody business that is of yours?" he demanded.

"It's quite simple. You have an unmarried son who will inherit your title someday, and I an unmarried daughter who quite soon will have more money than she can possibly spend."

It was silent in the room except for the crackling of the fire in the hearth. At last the Duke replied and this time there was a trace of amusement in his voice. "So—you wish Monty to marry your daughter?"

"Exactly."

"As you appear to be well-informed regarding my affairs, what do you know of my son?" the Duke inquired.

Samuel Templeton replied with cynicism. "Not much, I fear, that is admirable. I understand the Marquess of Medford is extremely handsome. I believe the word used to describe him was 'debonair.' He did surprisingly well at Oxford, but aside from that doesn't appear to have much to recommend him—the typical idle, restless young English aristocrat who divides his time between women of a rather questionable reputation and gambling at his club or the races. Also during the past few years he has managed to squander a considerable amount of the family fortune, to the point where I've been told that very shortly he will be forced to sell his string of horses. On the strength of all this, the thought crossed my mind he might welcome a reprieve."

"And after such a devastating description, you would consider him an acceptable suitor for your daughter?" The Duke's voice revealed his amazement.

"Certainly, for he can give her what I desire—a title and an impregnable position in society."

As the Duke was about to reply, his host raised his hand peremptorily. "Hear me out," he said. Atherton, struck by the force and authority in his voice, could well understand how easily he was able to dominate a board meeting.

"I am getting old," Templeton continued in a more conciliatory tone. "And I'm not well. I have all the money and all the power I've ever wanted. My wife died six years ago and when I die, Maria will be left completely alone. She is very young, only eighteen, and has led a sheltered life. It is imperative that she be protected. Besides"—he hesitated for a moment and his eyes flashed with sudden anger—"I've always had a hankering to break into London society. You're a tight little group, Sir. My wife and I were in London several times, and nobody but a few of my business associates paid us the slightest attention. You probably will not remember, as it was obviously inconsequential as far as you were concerned, but I do. I had a letter of introduction delivered to you and your family. You never answered it. In fact, the Duchess even failed to ask my wife to tea. I never forget an insult."

"I'm sorry. I fear I don't recall the incident." The Duke relaxed a bit and relit his cigar. He was beginning to enjoy himself and felt there was no harm in listening to the rest of this strange man's preposterous plan. He could always refuse. In fact, it would give him immense delight to do so.

"What I have in mind is a contract—an iron-clad contract. Your son woos my daughter and wins her. At that time, money will be available to you which will restore your fortune, repair your property, and allow you to continue living in your usual style. I will only require one thing in return—that my daughter is firmly established in society as the Marchioness of Medford. Your son can continue to gamble, if he wishes, continue to engage in his tawdry little affairs. I understand all that is perfectly acceptable in your circle, and I'm willing, too, to look the other way, as long as my daughter's position remains intact. Well, what do you say?" He poured more brandy and sat down in his chair once more, staring at his guest with an air of impatience.

The Duke sat lost in thought, gazing into the fire. After recovering from the unpleasant shock of discovering that Samuel Templeton was completely aware of the critical condition of his affairs, he began to think that perhaps this offer, instead of being a ridiculous plan, might prove a miraculous opportunity to extricate himself from disaster. Was it such an outlandish idea after all? And as he began to place it within the realm of possibility, he decided it would be foolhardy to flatly reject the offer merely to have the satisfaction of snubbing his host.

How wonderful it would be to live out his remaining days on his estate without the constant threat of bankruptcy, of ending his life in poverty and disgrace! And in addition wasn't it high time his indolent son made some sacrifice to save the family name? All things considered, was it really such a bizarre proposition?

"Well . . . ," Samuel Templeton was scowling.

The Duke looked up at his host and saw by his expression that this was a one-time offer which would be swiftly withdrawn if he became adamant.

"I am tempted to say yes," he finally conceded, "but, of course, I can't answer for my son."

The clock on the mantel boomed out the hour of midnight and Samuel Templeton rose. "I think he could be persuaded, and on the strength of that belief, I've already rented a house for the season in London, in Grosvenor Square. I plan to arrive there with my daughter by the end of April —a good time to settle in and perhaps spend a weekend or two in the country before the Coronation. Upon your return, I would suggest you talk it over with your son and then send me a cable. You might simply say 'Barkis is willing.'" **He** laughed heartily. "I like that touch, don't you?"

The Duke did not answer, again deep in thought. "It is intriguing," he said at last. "Damn intriguing. But what about your daughter? How will she react to all of this?"

"My daughter will know nothing of our plan. She will go to London and be so overwhelmed by your son's attentions that she will fall desperately in love. But as for the contract, which we will sign, she must know nothing about it . . . nothing."

"And if she doesn't fall in love?" the Duke asked. "What then?"

Samuel Templeton shrugged his shoulders. "That is your son's problem, not mine, but from what I've heard about him he should not find it a difficult task. He appears to be without peer in the art of romance."

The Duke of Atherton sighed as he rose. "That is true," he replied. "Do you have a picture of your daughter I could take to Monty? That's quite in order, you know. The kings always received pictures of prospective brides before reaching a decision." He shuddered slightly, thinking of Anne of Cleves.

Samuel Templeton strode to his massive desk

and, picking up a miniature, handed it over to the Duke. "It's all I have. Taken several years ago."

The Duke studied the photograph of a very young girl astride her pony. She was thin and scrawny, her pale face dominated by huge dark eyes.

"It will have to do." For the first time Samuel Templeton sounded slightly apologetic. "She's no beauty but then she's not ugly either."

The Duke pocketed the miniature without comment and stretched out his hand to his host. "Agreed," he said cheerfully. "Early in the evening I called you mad, and I still consider you so, but I find your plan irresistible. To put it bluntly, I am on the verge of bankruptcy and you have thrown me a lifeline. As soon as I arrive in London, I'll have a talk with Monty and cable you his answer."

"And when the betrothal is announced, we'll hammer out the contract."

Samuel Templeton moved towards the door and the Duke of Atherton followed him into the hallway where a servant in black livery waited with his cloak.

"My coachman will drive you to the Waldorf." Samuel Templeton and the Duke of Atherton shook hands, and as the Duke stepped outside into a cold, rainy March night, he wondered if the unusual interview had actually occurred, or if he would awaken later in his hotel room only to discover he had been dreaming.

toast with butter accompanying it—she cast about in her mind for something to say to Sir John. But

CHAPTER TWO

Miss Munson's Academy for Young Ladies was situated on the east bank of the Hudson River, affording a spectacular view of the Palisades. At one time the property of a robber baron who had been foolish enough to tangle with a Vanderbilt, it was a palatial stone structure—an exact replica of a French chateau in Lombardy—surrounded by vast lawns, formal gardens, greenhouses, and stables.

Presently it was the temporary residence of fifty young girls who had been packed off by their wealthy parents to acquire poise, polish, and if time permitted, an education.

Maria Templeton stood at the window of her tower room watching the evening shadows lengthen on a lawn still brown and covered here and there with patches of snow. On the river a steamboat plowed northward, black soot from its funnels smudging the pale blue sky. The New York to Albany night boat was on time, its bright lights flinging a necklace of gold on the darkening waters.

It was the end of her sixth year at Miss Munson's and, since for some time Maria Templeton had considered it her home, she viewed the familiar scene beneath her window with deep sadness, reluctant to acknowledge that the time to leave was drawing near.

Graduation was in June. What then, she asked herself? Undoubtedly the summer would be spent at Lake Placid under the watchful eyes of a housekeeper and a bevy of servants. But after that, what plans would her father have in store? With a sigh she crossed to a scarred desk piled high with books and opened one only to close it with a bang. Reaching for pen and paper, she started a letter to her father.

"Dear Father," it began, "Graduation Day has been set for the tenth of June. I do hope you will be able to attend. I believe I have won the English prize and there is a good chance I'll be at the top of my class, so it would be wonderful to have you present when I receive my awards.

"Recently I have been giving a good deal of

thought to the future. I would like very much to attend college next fall. Miss Munson believes I would have no difficulty gaining admission to Vassar or Wellesley. Please let me know your reaction."

Interrupted by a gentle tap at her door, she sang out, "Come in!" It was one of the maids in a crisp black uniform with starched white collar and cuffs and a stiff lace cap on her head.

"You're wanted in the office, Miss," she said and with a puzzled frown Maria smoothed her hair and dress before following the maid down stone steps leading to the ground floor.

It was unusual to be summoned to Miss Munson's quarters after supper time, and she was seized with panic, with a dreadful premonition that something terrible had occurred. It had been on a night like this almost six years ago that Miss Munson had informed her of her mother's death.

Adelaide Munson, a formidable woman under any circumstances, was particularly so when one was ushered into her dark paneled inner sanctum, forced to cross what seemed to be a tremendously long distance from the door to a leather chair placed beside her desk.

As always, she was tightly laced in a long black dress, a diamond brooch glistening on her ample bosom, the only relief to the starkness of her apparel. Her luxuriant white hair, swept up into a myriad of curls on the top of her head, gave her a majestic look and emphasized the cold glint of her blue eyes.

Watching the slender girl's entrance, Adelaide Munson felt a slight flicker of sympathy that Maria's presence always seemed to invoke. She was so small, so vulnerable and, during the six years she had spent at the school, Miss Munson had felt more protective towards her than any other student.

She felt protective but annoyed too—annoyed at a father who was so engrossed with his vast holdings that he seemed to feel sending off his daughter to a first-rate boarding school fulfilled his parental obligations. Each winter since his wife's death he had requested that Maria spend the Christmas holidays at the school, and she had been the only student left in the dormitory—a lonely existence for one so young.

Miss Munson smiled at Maria Templeton and, motioning to a letter on her desk, came directly to the point. "I received word from your father this afternoon. He wants you to leave here immediately. Apparently he plans to take you on a trip abroad, to England."

"Now? Before the end of the term?" Maria's voice contained a note of panic. "But I don't want to go, Miss Munson. I want to stay here until June."

"I'm aware of that, my dear," Miss Munson

spoke soothingly. "And we'll be sorry to have you leave. I'm sure you realize you've been an excellent addition to our student body. But it's only a matter of missing a few months here, and think how fortunate you'll be to arrive in London in time for the Coronation."

She studied the slender girl almost lost in the big leather chair and sighed. Somehow it was difficult to picture this quiet, serious child, who appeared closer to sixteen than eighteen, caught up in the whirlwind of court receptions and balls. She would be like a little sparrow lost among a flock of birds of colorful plumage. Miss Munson, an avid reader of the activities of the social set in London, was often shocked but nevertheless fascinated by its frivolity, and found it impossible to picture Maria Templeton participating. How would she ever manage to survive?

The large dark eyes of the young girl, sad and haunted, touched her deeply and, rising from her chair, she crossed over to Maria and rested a hand on her shoulder, for her a most unusual gesture.

"We'll miss you dreadfully, my child. But then I think it's time you had a chance to become better acquainted with your father. Now you must go and pack, for tomorrow Jonathan will drive you to the station to catch the early morning train."

Maria Templeton stood up slowly. Over the years she had learned by the tone of Miss Munson's voice when an interview had ended. "Thank you, Miss Munson. I'll miss you too." She hesitated briefly and then plunged onward. "But what about graduation, and college? When you called for me I was in the midst of writing my father asking for permission to continue my studies next fall."

"You'll receive your diploma, of course. No question of that," Miss Munson said easily. "As for college, why not let the matter rest for a while until you have an opportunity to discuss it with your father?"

Seeing that the girl was on the verge of tears, she stood up quickly and opened the door. "I'll say good-bye in the morning, my dear," she said briskly.

As she watched Maria's departure, Miss Munson thought she moved with unusual grace but then it was almost impossible to tell in her school uniform, a shapeless navy-blue jumper, whether the girl had a good figure or not. The headmistress was at a loss to visualize how Maria would look in a ball gown or an afternoon frock. She almost called out to her to come back for a cup of tea and cake, but long years of discipline restrained the impulse.

When Maria reached her room in the tower, she crumpled the note to her father with one fierce gesture and allowed the tears she had managed to hold back in the presence of Miss Munson to flow freely. For the first time in her life she experienced an upsurge of anger towards her father, anger because he moved her about like an ivory piece on a chessboard, an inanimate object completely devoid of emotions, desires, or the ability to think.

"I won't go," she cried out defiantly to the empty room, knowing even as she spoke the words that she had no choice.

The Conqueror took three weeks to cross the storm-tossed Atlantic. As Samuel Templeton was fond of saying, it was even larger and more luxurious than the *Victoria and Albert*. While the *Victoria and Albert* carried a crew of three hundred, *The Conqueror* had three hundred and twenty-five members. And while thirty servants in scarlet livery answered to their Majesties' slightest whims, Templeton's yacht had thirty-five domestics dressed in dark green uniforms always at his beck and call.

Templeton selected the first night out as the most propitious moment to begin to become acquainted with his daughter. Having an analytical turn of mind, before meeting her in the dining salon, he ran over several questions he would ask her.

"Well, at least you're a good sailor," he said jovially as footmen pulled out their chairs with grave formality.

Glancing about the large room with an air of

approval, he decided he had been wise to have it simply decorated. Quietly elegant by candlelight, its white paneled walls were the proper background for his first-rate French Impressionist paintings. At the head of the highly polished mahogany table, which could easily seat thirty guests, he stared at his daughter, who sat silently, looking frail and lost in a huge carved armchair, her white silk gown accentuating the brilliance of her dark eyes.

"We're going to Paris first," he said, unfolding his napkin. "I sense your clothes are all wrong. Although I'm no expert on women's fashions, I'm certain they are not what ladies in society are wearing."

She flushed and glanced down quickly at her dress which was severely cut without ornamentation. "It's what we wore at Miss Munson's when we dressed for dinner," she protested mildly.

"Yes, yes, I'm sure it was completely proper for that occasion, but I'll take you to Worth's when we arrive in Paris and we'll purchase the latest fashions."

He tackled his oyster soup with relish and the chilled chablis that accompanied it, casting about for another topic of conversation.

"With your diploma, Miss Munson sent me a detailed report of your accomplishments," he began. "I was glad to learn you are considered an expert horsewoman."

Maria flushed again and as she smiled, her father noted that her face lit up with an inner radiance that made her quite attractive. Why she's close to being pretty, he decided with some amazement, and perhaps with the proper clothes, she'll be able to hold her own.

"I love to ride," she replied. "My happiest moments have always been on horseback. We had a wonderful instructor and there wasn't a jump I didn't learn to take."

"Splendid, and I also note you had four years of French."

"I speak it fluently."

The servants removed the soup plates and brought in the second course.

"And dancing?" he asked. "What about dancing?"

For the first time Maria laughed a warm lilting laugh. "Oh, we learned to dance at Miss Munson's," she replied. "All of the important steps from the valse to the mazurka, but I have to confess I've never danced with a man."

Samuel Templeton raised his thick eyebrows in astonishment. "Never danced with a man? Unbelievable! I'm afraid you have me confused."

"There were no men at Miss Munson's," Maria explained patiently. "Ever." And her eyes sparkled as she found to her surprise that she was enjoying herself. "With the exception, of course, of the riding master and the men who stoked the furnaces and took care of the grounds. No, we girls danced together, one-two-three-glide, one-two-three-glide around and around the huge gymnasium, wearing our white middy blouses and navy-blue bloomers. We must have been quite a sight. So I learned to lead as well as to follow."

Her father joined in her laughter and was relieved to see she possessed a sense of humor. "But that will never do," he replied with mock seriousness. "When you reach London you must remember to follow—always follow."

"I'll try," she promised, as with fascination she watched the butler at the sideboard slice the roast duck with expertise.

"And you must grow accustomed to wine," he added, pointing to the crystal glass which she had left untouched. As he spoke she obediently took a sip.

"I found some of the subjects you selected rather strange," he continued after an awkward silence. "Economics—now why in the world would a young girl study economics? I'm amazed Miss Munson allowed it in her curriculum."

"Miss Munson's school was in some ways very avant-garde," his daughter remarked. "Although the subject of men was forbidden, we were offered a wide variety of courses. In fact, Father, before your letter arrived, I was about to write you to ask if next year I could attend college."

Her father dropped his fork and gazed at her

in astonishment. "Don't tell me I've spawned a bluestocking," he exclaimed. "My dear child, if so, I've rescued you in the nick of time. Where we are going you must not talk about economics or politics or anything else that could be classified as serious."

"Then what shall I talk about?" Their eyes met and he noticed that her lips, full and sensuous like his, were parted in an amused smile.

"Well, I'm not quite certain. You see, I've never really taken the time to be exposed to what is called 'society.' But I'm sure young ladies address themselves to such subjects as the latest fashions and who danced with whom at last night's ball. And they gossip—I'm positive they gossip."

She frowned. "I hate idle gossip, Father," she protested. "Do you suppose I'll be a wallflower? Someone whom no one asks to dance?"

He sampled the rosé the butler had poured, nodding his head in approval and then belatedly realized she was waiting for his reply.

"Of course not." He spoke heartily. "Why, it's inconceivable that the daughter of Samuel Templeton could be anything but a success at whatever she undertakes."

He returned to concentrating on the wine, and as he lifted his glass to his lips, he recalled the cable the Duke of Atherton had sent him shortly after his return to England, and smiled. It had amused him greatly that the Duke had added two words to the message that had been originally suggested. "Barkis is more than willing," it had read, with the "more" in capital letters.

Maria noted the smile on her father's face and wondered what he was finding so amusing. Since her headlong departure from Miss Munson's Academy, she had had time to puzzle over the reason why her father had summoned her from obscurity, ordering her to accompany him to Europe.

Well aware that he was a man with a reputation for rapid decisions, for impetuosity, it nevertheless seemed strange for him to embark on a trip that would embroil him in the social scene—a scene he had always studiously ignored.

Was it possible, she speculated, that he had taken this step to consummate some business venture, or maybe, just maybe, had he developed a case of remorse regarding the responsibilities he owed to his daughter? Had the journey been born solely from concern for her?

She recognized that he was a complicated man and therefore it would probably be best not to attempt to analyze his motives but rather to accept the situation and consider it an opportunity to establish a closer rapport. Later she could again bring up the subject of attending college in the fall. "Bluestocking!" that's what he had called her. And what, she concluded, was wrong with being that!

The long days at sea drew them closer together.

Her father was delighted to discover that she played a keen game of chess, and they whiled away many hours attempting to outwit each other. Brisk walks each day on deck and leisurely dinners together made the voyage, despite wind, rain, and rolling seas, a most pleasant venture.

Maria Templeton's memories of Paris were exceedingly limited, for she had been there only once when she was six and had spent most of that time in the park with her nurse. To her delight she found this visit completely different.

From the moment they debarked from *The Conqueror* at Cherbourg until they entered the Hotel Meurice, she stepped into an entirely new environment, strange but nevertheless exciting.

They dined in their suite that night and the following morning she was escorted by her father to Worth's, where he gave explicit instructions to have her outfitted in every conceivable type of costume she might need for the London season.

Overwhelmed by the huge salon with its ornate mirrors, damask wallpaper, and ceiling lamps of crimson silk, she was shown the entire collection from simple morning dresses to extravagant ball gowns, fashioned in soft velvets and delicate satins, intricately decorated with lace, tulle, and precious gems. I'll surely trip on the long trains, she thought nervously, feeling awkward and gauche in the midst of such splendor.

It took two weeks of lengthy fittings to complete her extensive wardrobe, and she had to admit she was more comfortable in the perfectly tailored black riding habit and a tweed suit for walks in the country than in the fabulous evening outfits and diaphanous tea gowns she had selected.

In the afternoons when her father was involved in business meetings, she ventured forth on her own, guidebook in hand, visiting the Louvre, Notre Dame, and the countless other sights of Paris. She found herself particularly enthralled with the bookstalls along the Seine and the busy market place, Les Halles.

By the end of the second week their suite overflowed with boxes of every conceivable size and shape and two huge trunks were delivered to contain her new wardrobe.

"I've engaged a French maid for you," her father informed her one morning at breakfast. "She'll do all the packing and be on hand whenever you need assistance in dressing. I think you'll like her. She's young but has impeccable references."

The next day Maria met Yvette and knew from the first moment that she would be not only a maid but a companion as well. She was a tiny blonde, pert, smart, and full of enthusiasm. "It is so nice," she exclaimed, "to be working for a young mistress. My last lady was old and crotchety and never went anywhere but to the opera." Spellbound by Maria's sumptuous wardrobe, she handled the exquisite gowns and fragile lingerie with infinite care.

On their last night in Paris, Maria prepared to accompany her father to Maxim's. It was to be their first evening out since during their stay they had eaten their meals in their suite.

"Sort of a trial run," Maria said to Yvette with a tremulous smile, hoping fervently she would live up to the occasion. After some consideration she selected a rose satin gown to wear. It had a short train and the skirt and bodice were scattered with tiny seed pearls.

Sitting at her dressing table, she began to brush her hair with shaking fingers and Yvette standing behind her finally said, "Let me do it for you, Mademoiselle. I think I know exactly how it should be."

Maria sighed gratefully, surrendering the brush. "If you only would, Yvette. I always comb it straight back and fasten it with a barrette. I know that isn't the way it should be worn but still I don't want it piled high with all those silly contraptions I've seen some of the ladies in Paris wearing."

"No, Mademoiselle, you are very young, so you should have your hair dressed simply. Those outlandish styles are for the older women. It makes the gentlemen concentrate on the head instead of the face and that way not notice the wrinkles. But you, Mademoiselle, are far too young for wrinkles so the hair should be merely a frame for your smooth skin and lovely eyes."

"Are my eyes lovely?" Maria asked in surprise. "I've always thought they were far too big."

"Wait and see, Mademoiselle," Yvette spoke soothingly and went to work with combs and brushes. "Your hair is curly and very thick. You should not pull it back so severely," she commented, brushing the luxuriant black hair until it fell into glossy waves around her face, and then fashioning soft curls that tumbled to her white shoulders.

"See how charming you look?" Yvette exclaimed. "Now wear the pearl necklace your father gave you and with a cluster of roses in your hair, I defy anyone to outshine you tonight."

Ready to leave, Maria slipped a silken cape lined with sable about her shoulders and took one last look in the mirror. A stranger stared back at her and she shook her head slowly, slightly bewildered.

"Yes, Mademoiselle, it is really you," Yvette said with a smile. "And you are lovely."

Maria turned to her swiftly and gave the startled maid an impetuous hug. "Oh, thank you, Yvette," she cried. "Thank you very, very much."

As she opened her bedroom door and stepped hesitantly into the drawing room, her father, who had been ready for some time and was staring restlessly out of the window, turned to greet her and caught his breath in astonishment. "My dear," he said gently. "Worth's and Yvette have wrought a miracle."

Maria laughed lightly and gave him a deep, formal curtsey. "Miss Munson would never recognize me. In fact I find it difficult to recognize myself. I'm very happy, Father, for I have been so fearful of embarrassing you in London."

"Embarrass me? That you could never do." He reached out his arm to her in a gallant gesture, tall and prepossessing in his perfectly tailored evening clothes. "And now on to Maxim's," he said. "But I consider it a shame you don't have a young man to escort you. However, that will all change, I'm sure, when we reach London."

They stepped from the hotel into a world of glamour that up until then Maria had never dreamed existed: Afterwards she could not recall what they had been served. She only knew that the food had been superb. But she always remembered vividly the table set with fragile china and sparkling crystal, the ice bucket of champagne beside them, the popping of golden corks, and above all the women, exquisitely dressed, supremely at ease, accompanied by men who she was certain must be most important personages—princes, grand dukes, and prominent diplomats at the very least.

Her father recognized a few and, pointing them

out to her, explained that Maxim's catered only to the elite and that Edward VII, when Prince of Wales, had dined there on his frequent trips to Paris.

"He has had many love affairs," her father remarked with a smile. "And Paris has undoubtedly been the longest lasting of them all."

As one course after another was placed before them, the scene to Maria became a colorful pageant with she, as a member of the audience, watching the actors and actresses perform. The band in crimson coats, playing their intoxicating music, became a background to the rise and fall of cultured voices and the frequent bursts of muted laughter.

It was over far too soon. As they drove in their carriage back to the hotel, Maria breathed in deeply the cool air of the spring night and understood for the first time why Paris was considered the city for lovers. Even the clop of the horses' hoofs on the pavement seemed to beat out a song of enchantment and she doubted if she would find anything in London to match the magic of this night.

With feelings of regret and trepidation on Maria's part, they crossed the Channel to Southampton the next day, arriving in London long after darkness had descended.

CHAPTER THREE

The house on Grosvenor Square was a massive structure with an overwhelming facade, a graceless potpourri of Georgian Revival, Victorian, and Neoclassic. Five stories high, it flaunted a bewildering array of bow, arched, and square windows, and at its peak a frieze of sculpture that lacked any particular merit. A tall wrought-iron fence screened the entrance from the street and in the rear a walled garden provided quiet and seclusion.

Inside the spacious rooms, overcrowded with heavy pieces of dark furniture, were thick oriental carpets and velvet draperies. The house had been staffed with twenty servants, and they found everything in perfect order upon their arrival.

To her relief, Maria discovered that her suite was tastefully and simply decorated in soft blues and white with its windows overlooking the garden.

In the mews behind the house lay the stables and coach house and Maria was touched to learn that her father had purchased a magnificent chestnut mare for her so she could go riding in Hyde Park.

The next morning in the sunny breakfast room she found Samuel Templeton in an extremely affable mood. "Already we have an invitation for the weekend," he remarked with obvious satisfaction. "To the Duke of Atherton's country place." He gestured towards a thick creamy envelope lying on the table beside his plate. "It's in Essex. A magnificent estate I've been told."

"Will many people be there?" she asked apprehensively.

"Oh, yes, there are sure to be. You'll like his lordship. I met him in New York not so long ago, and I consider it most courteous of him to include us in his house party."

Finishing his coffee, he pushed back his chair and rose abruptly. "Now I have business in the city, but I expect you'll be occupied deciding what clothes to take on Friday. We'll go by train and of course Yvette will accompany you." Halfway out of the room he turned back and patted her on the shoulder awkwardly. "It's a beautiful day. Why not try out your horse in the park? But be sure to have one of the grooms along."

After he had departed, she lingered at the breakfast table for a while, staring out at the garden with its patch of green lawn and its brick pathway bordered by yellow daffodils. To her dismay she discovered that the newly born confidence she had gained that evening at Maxim's had completely vanished to be replaced by an overwhelming certainty that a weekend at a splendid house in the country would somehow spell disaster.

How dreadful it would be, she thought, if she said and did all the wrong things—not so much for herself but for her father, who for some reason seemed so terribly anxious that she should be a success. To her joy she had discovered during the trip across the Atlantic and the brief stay in Paris that a rapport had been established between them that had never existed before. Now she was fearful that this closeness, which had become so important, would vanish if she disappointed him.

Sighing deeply, she left the breakfast room and, after wandering restlessly through the house, decided that perhaps a ride in the Park might dissipate her gloomy forebodings.

Changing into her black riding habit and placing a smart derby hat on her head, she crossed through the garden to the mews and watched as one of the grooms saddled the horses.

She had filched a few lumps of sugar from the kitchen, and, before mounting the magnificent chestnut, Sabrina, treated her to some sugar and stroked her glossy mane. Maria was glad to see she was spirited, anxious to be exercised, and it took all of her skill to keep the horse at a walk as they started out in the direction of Hyde Park.

Reaching Rotten Row, she understood why it was considered one of the sights of England, for they entered a dazzling scene. It was a glorious day, warm and sunny, and with her groom beside her she trotted along the wide avenue, passing other riders and vehicles of every description—landaus, victorias, and yellow and cream traps. The coachmen were wearing cockades and the footmen were turned out in smart livery, while along the paths women in sweeping gowns strolled leisurely by, protecting their lovely faces from the sun by gay colored parasols.

Maria found it completely entrancing and was thankful her father had had the foresight to see she was properly attired. Her riding habit was exactly right. Her groom, a young man in his twenties, was enjoying the excursion too. "The King often drives here," he told her, "but I don't see him so far today."

Slowing their horses to a walk, they drew alongside a bright yellow trap drawn by a tandem and

Maria studied the occupants with interest. The woman wore a long blue gown with insets of lace at the shoulders and about the neck. Her floppy picture hat of the same color was adorned with graceful plumes of white feathers and as her wide gray eyes met Maria's for an instant before glancing away, Maria realized she was seeing for the first time one of those famous London beauties so much discussed in newspapers and magazines. Her lips were parted in a provocative smile and her golden hair glistened in the warm spring sunlight.

The man beside her was attired in morning clothes and, as Maria and her groom rode by, he raised his top hat to them in a jaunty salute, and she caught a glimpse of the most handsome young man she had ever encountered. His curly hair was a startling red, his eyes as brilliant as the blue of the Mediterranean, and his smile seemed to hold a promise that every moment in his company would be one of delight.

"Who are they?" she asked her groom impulsively as soon as they were out of earshot.

A slight smile flickered across the boy's face. "The gentleman is the Marquess of Medford. But I don't recognize his companion." There was something in the tone of his voice when he pronounced the word "companion" that made Maria wonder if the stunning woman in the bright yellow trap could be one of those actresses mentioned in hushed tones who became the companions and often mistresses of young men about town. Unbeknownst to the headmistress and her staff of teachers, the young girls at Miss Munson's Academy frequently wiled away the lonely evenings devouring the scandal sheets that were daringly purchased on their infrequent trips to New York and hidden carefully during the day under their mattresses.

I wonder if she's a Gaiety Girl, Maria speculated, admiring her beauty and at the same time envying her for being in the company of such an attractive man.

The next morning, when she rode once more along Rotten Row, she found herself searching for the yellow trap, hoping for another glimpse of the beautiful woman with her dashing escort and feeling strangely disappointed when she did not encounter them again.

Maria spent Thursday in a frenzy of packing and on Friday morning she was amazed by the mounds of luggage stacked in the front hallway.

After luncheon she and her father, accompanied by Yvette and Robert, her father's valet, departed for Paddington Station. It was another perfect spring day and Maria enjoyed the train ride through the peaceful English countryside despite the fact that every click of the wheels on the track brought her closer to a weekend that by now she was beginning to view with considerable panic.

In the late afternoon, their train pulled into the village of Eaton, and they descended onto a platform crammed with guests and formidable piles of luggage, from jewel boxes to gun cases to trunks of every conceivable size.

Outside of the station the carriages were lined up waiting, and the Templetons were escorted to a victoria. Sitting beside her father, Maria watched with interest as the elegantly clad ladies and gentlemen were assigned to the various vehicles while the servants efficiently sorted out the baggage and climbed into sturdy wagons equipped with narrow wooden seats.

In a matter of moments order replaced chaos and they were on their way, passing swiftly through the village and on to the country road that wound its way to Longacres, the Duke of Atherton's country estate.

As they passed between stone pillars which marked the entrance and swept down a wide avenue lined with stately trees, Maria caught her first glimpse of the house—a huge rambling structure of gray stone with square turrets, its red-brown roofs sprinkled with innumerable chimney pots. A red and blue flag in the courtyard fluttered in the breeze, and, disturbed by the clatter of approaching carriages, a covey of white pigeons became airborne, circling above them.

The carriages entered the paved courtyard and

powdered footmen in red velvet breeches and black jackets waited outside the carved oak doorway. As Maria stepped down, she was overwhelmed by the size of the building. "There must be at least a hundred rooms," she murmured to her father.

"At least," he replied.

There was a towering structure directly in front of them with two long wings on either side. Impressive, Maria concluded, but somehow cold and forbidding. Shivering despite the warmth of the afternoon sun, she was ushered inside to be greeted by her hostess, the Duchess of Atherton.

"My dear, we have been looking forward with pleasure to your visit," the Duchess exclaimed and Maria had a brief impression of a tall, imposing woman with snow-white hair, a cool clipped voice and a rather frigid smile. Not unlike Miss Munson, Maria thought, as she followed a footman two flights up the marble staircase and along an endless number of corridors and dark, narrow passageways.

At last the footman stopped in front of a door and she realized they had finally reached their destination. She discovered her name neatly printed on a white card that had been slipped into a tiny brass frame fastened to the paneling.

As she stepped inside, the footman mumbled, "Tea is being served in the drawing room," and then departed.

It was a large square room with high vaulted ceilings, and Maria wondered as she looked about how many generations of Atherton guests had slept here in the huge four-poster bed with its pale silken covers. Moving about, she was particularly entranced by the writing table, where she found a gilt-edged card listing the times of the post's arrival and departure and the hours when meals would be served.

Fingering the thick vellum writing paper with the name "Longacres" engraved in discreet lettering under a ducal coronet, she was sorry there was no one she could think of to whom she wanted to write.

She found books on the satinwood night table by her bedside and smiled as she read the titles—all romantic novels obviously selected with the thought that they would appeal to a young girl.

On her dressing table she discovered a corsage of delicate spring violets and to her amazement she noted that the cozy which covered the metal hot water canister on the washstand had the family crest embroidered upon it.

Remembering that the footman had muttered something about tea, she washed her face, combed her hair quickly and decided it would be quite a challenge to venture forth in search of the drawing room. After a few trials and errors, she found it on the second floor and stood in the doorway hesitating, reluctant to step inside.

Before her was a lively scene. The Duchess of Atherton, seated on a love seat by the fireplace, was presiding over the silver tea service, while footmen in their scarlet livery moved among the guests with platters of scones, wafer-thin sandwiches and assorted cakes.

It was a tremendous room and Maria noticed that practically every table was crammed with photographs in silver frames. Curious to examine them more closely but fearful of doing so, she glanced quickly at one as she entered the room. It was a picture of Edward VII with his signature scrawled across it.

Her father was standing by the fireplace balancing a delicate tea cup, and as he saw her approach beckoned to her to join him. He was engaged in conversation with a tall aristocratic gentleman in country tweeds who broke off what he was saying to turn towards her as she drew near. She was introduced to the Duke of Atherton.

"Splendid that you could come," he said and, as she gave him a quick curtsey, she felt that he was studying her with an inordinate amount of interest. "But I'm afraid you'll find us all far too ancient, except, of course, for my son who is somewhere about. I believe he went riding."

Slender for a man of his age, he was without question lord of the manor, and as he smiled at her she detected a measure of warmth in his rather prominent gray eyes.

"Maria is accustomed to being with older people," her father inserted smoothly. "She's been looking forward to this weekend as much as I."

His lordship escorted her to the tea table where the Duchess languidly poured a cup of tea, and then, holding her arm lightly, he guided her around the room introducing her to the other guests. Stately women in traveling costumes greeted her briefly, their menfolk bowing. Soon completely confused by the number of titled names, she wondered if she was being presented to the entire hierarchy of British society.

After tea everyone retired to their rooms and Maria found Yvette already at work unpacking her valises.

"Time for a nap and a bath," Yvette said to her mistress, pointing to a metal tub that had been placed in front of the fire. "I've never been in such a tremendous place in all my life. It took me ten minutes to come here from the servants' quarters." She giggled. "We had tea too, Robert and I, but because Mr. Templeton is not titled we were seated at the farthest end of the table from the housekeeper."

"Below the salt? Do they really follow protocol to that extent?" Maria asked in amazement.

"They certainly do. But never mind, Mademoiselle, I was glad to be next to Robert. He's very nice. Not pompous like so many of the servants." As she chattered away, she poured large cans of hot water into the tub. "Now hop in quickly," she directed. "Even with a fire in the hearth the room is damp and chilly."

After her bath Maria slipped between the pink silken sheets and fell immediately asleep. When she awakened, she lay there quietly for a while watching Yvette light the lamps and lay out her clothes.

"I thought the white satin would be appropriate, Mademoiselle," Yvette said when she saw her mistress was awake. "That, with your mother's diamond necklace and bracelet and violets in your hair should be a perfect costume for a spring evening."

Maria yawned, agreeing, and with Yvette's help dressed for dinner. Sparkling rhinestones were scattered on the full skirt of the white satin gown she was wearing and, although it was not as décolleté as evening dresses had been in the Victorian period, it still showed off her smooth white shoulders and slender neck to advantage. Yvette fastened the violets in her hair, making a small crown amidst her lustrous curls, and Maria, smiling at her reflection in the mirror, was satisfied with the result.

As she entered the drawing room the guests were being served sherry, and Maria, accepting a glass from one of the footmen, found her eyes drawn to the only other young person present. He stood by one of the long windows, talking to her father and an elderly gentleman she had met at tea—Sir John Hetherington she believed was his name, a neighbor of the Duke of Atherton.

But it was the young man who engaged her attention. Surely she had seen him before. And then she remembered her morning ride along Rotten Row and the handsome youth with the bright red hair and jaunty smile seated in the yellow trap. So the Duke's son was the Marquess of Medford.

As she drifted across the room towards them, she recalled the lovely blonde who had ridden beside him and the feeling of intimacy she had sensed existing between them, and her spirits took a little plunge of disappointment. Surely, she thought, he will find my company a dreadful letdown.

As she approached them, the young man met her glance and gave her that wonderful warm smile which she had found so entrancing that morning in Rotten Row.

"This must be your daughter," he said to Samuel Templeton, bowing to Maria gracefully and extending his hand. "You've met Sir John, I believe?"

Maria nodded and smiled at the elderly gentleman, who this afternoon she had ticketed as a rather tedious individual, probably totally lacking in a sense of humor. Now as she curtsied to him, she saw that his faded blue eyes under bushy white eyebrows contained a twinkle of amusement.

"We were discussing horses, Miss Templeton," he said in a quavery voice. "Do you by any chance enjoy attending the races?"

"I never have attended." Maria sipped her sherry. "But as I'm fond of riding, I'm sure I'd enjoy watching a race."

"Good," the Marquess of Medford replied. "I'm glad to hear that you ride. If you wish I'll show you the stables the first thing tomorrow."

The guests were beginning to move out of the drawing room and down the grand staircase, and Sir John Hetherington, finishing his sherry, stretched out his arm to Maria. "I believe I'm to take you in to dinner," he said.

The chandeliers in the magnificent dining room twinkled like stars above the long table which glistened with silverware and crystal goblets. A footman stood behind each chair. Maria guessed there must be thirty of them at the table. She was seated between Sir John and the Viscount of Selby, a short, stocky middle-aged man with a ruddy complexion, who said a cool "good-evening" to her and then became completely absorbed in conversation with a striking woman seated on his other side.

As the first course was served—beluga caviar on toast with vodka accompanying it—she cast about in her mind for something to say to Sir John. But soon, to her relief, as one course followed another, with a variety of wines and eventually champagne, she learned that talking to Sir John was not a problem. Forgetting her father's advice to avoid any serious subjects, they launched into a lively exchange over American politics. He asked for her opinion of Theodore Roosevelt, and she was surprised to discover he knew as much about the man as she did.

"Do you approve of his attitude towards the trusts?" he asked.

Maria burst out laughing. "I shouldn't," she replied. "But I do. Please don't tell my father though, for I'm sure he would never forgive me."

By the time they had reached dessert, she had confided in him that she hoped to attend college the next year and to her surprise he nodded his head in satisfaction. "You have a good mind," he told her. "Use it."

She had never experienced such a lengthy dinner before and, when the Duchess finally rose and the ladies moved out of the dining room, leaving the men to their port, she estimated they had been at the table for close to two hours and had been served seven courses. She had been particularly intrigued by one, which Sir John explained to her was a specialty of Longacres, consisting of quail stuffed with ortolan, the ortolan stuffed with truffles, with pâté de foie gras as the final touch.

In the drawing room she joined the ladies. As she listened to their rather desultory exchanges, she experienced her first feeling of loneliness. Unquestionably, they were women from the highest strata of English society, but she found their discussions of the latest fashions and their preoccupation with tidbits of gossip stultifying.

Although occupied in discussing people and situations with which she was totally unfamiliar, Maria considered their remarks not only vacuous but frequently spiteful. Appalled by the general tone of the conversation, liberally sprinkled with "Can you imagine" and "How deevey," she witnessed the destruction of several reputations in the course of half an hour and concluded that scandalous behavior was perfectly acceptable in this tightly knit little society as long as it was contained within the group.

After such a tremendous banquet, she eventually became lulled by the rise and fall of their voices and found it impossible to suppress a yawn.

"Do you play bridge, my dear?" the Duchess asked, apparently at last realizing that no attempt had been made to include Maria in the conversation.

"I'm afraid not."

"Well, no matter." The Duchess shugged her shoulders, "I'm sure that Monty will entertain you."

During dinner Monty had sat across from her

smiling at her each time she glanced in his direction. Poor Monty, she thought, he's stuck with me whether he likes it or not, and her exchanges with Sir John, which she had found so stimulating, she suspected would not have interested the Marquess of Medford in the slightest degree.

After a seemingly endless time, the men rejoined the ladies. Card tables had already been set up in the drawing room and as the guests decided who would play with whom, Monty crossed over to her side.

"Do you play bridge?" he asked.

"No, I'm sorry I don't."

"Good," he replied. "As I find it tedious, suppose I show you around."

"I'd like that."

Reaching out a hand, he raised her to her feet. His fingers grasping hers were warm and strong to the touch and as she tipped back her head to smile up at him and he returned the smile, she was shocked to discover that emotions she never suspected she possessed rose to the surface and engulfed her.

Pulling her trembling hand away from his, she prayed that he had failed to notice how powerfully the impact of his personality had affected her. What a fool he must consider me, she thought, and in order to cover up her confusion, she called out to her father, "We'll be back soon," but he was already so deeply engrossed in his game that he acknowledged her remark with only a curt nod.

He led her to the gallery first where they inspected the large collection of oil paintings of generations of Athertons from the first Duke to the present one, along with portraits of their wives and children. Framed in ornate gold, it seemed to Maria as if they all stared down at her with disdain and disapproval.

"They're rather sure of themselves, aren't they?" he said with a laugh as they studied a portrait of his grandmother in her lavish court gown with a diamond tiara crowning her thick auburn hair.

"Yes, but why not? I don't suppose they had any reason to feel otherwise."

"You interested me greatly at dinner," he commented as they walked along the glistening parquet floor, their feet echoing hollowly in the vast room.

"How?" She gave him a puzzled glance.

"I've dined with Sir John countless times in the past, and I have never seen him carry on an animated conversation before. Usually he concentrates on the food and wine and later dozes off wearing a dour expression. What on earth were you talking about?"

"Politics."

"Politics!"

"Yes," Maria blushed. "He is an admirer of

Theodore Roosevelt and was asking all sorts of questions."

"Which you were able to answer?"

"Oh, yes. I find Roosevelt a fascinating man." She blushed again. "I hope Father didn't overhear us. He warned me before coming that ladies are not supposed to be interested in such things and that I should limit myself to lighter subjects."

Monty laughed. "Lighter subjects do seem to be the order of the day. Lord, you must have been dreadfully bored after dinner listening to the conversation in the drawing room."

"Much of it I didn't understand."

"Don't bother your head about it," he replied. "But I wager it revolved around Lady Sybil Gravestroke and her latest indiscretion. They would circle the subject, of course, never come out pointblank and say she was involved in a scandalous love affair. But there would be all sorts of innuendoes which would not be difficult to interpret even for one unfamiliar with London society."

They had reached the end of the gallery and went on to inspect the billiard room, the writing rooms, and then the library.

There was a fire crackling in the hearth and the Marquess of Medford stood with his back to it, an amused expression on his face as he watched her examine the large collection of beautifully bound books on the shelves.

"You like to read?" he asked.

"Oh, yes, very much and what a lovely room for it!" She glanced about her at the tremendous sofas facing each other by the hearth and the deep, comfortable chairs placed by the windows where the velvet draperies had been drawn, creating a warm and intimate atmosphere.

"Would you like some port or sherry?" He lifted a crystal decanter from a near-by table.

"Oh, no," she protested. "I've never had so much wine and champagne in all my life as I've had tonight. It's a miracle I'm not tipsy."

He motioned for her to sit down on one of the sofas and, pouring some port for himself, joined her there.

He has to be the most attractive man I've ever seen, she thought. It was not merely his striking red hair, blue eyes, and smooth complexion that made him so. It was everything about him—his smile, his voice, soft and assured, and the way he moved with nonchalance and grace.

"What do you do?" she asked abruptly.

As he sipped his drink his lips curved in a slight smile. He was clean-shaven except for a well-trimmed moustache. "Not much if you mean do I work. I finished at Oxford two years ago and much to everyone's amazement I was not sent down. I've had a few duties connected with my regiment but aside from that I guess you'd say

I've been idle. There's nothing to keep me occupied here on the estate—we have a most competent overseer and then it's my father's domain. I love the place though, every inch of it. So when I'm not at Longacres, hunting or fishing, I'm usually in London." He paused. "Surveying the social scene," he finished.

"Don't you sit in the House of Lords?"

"Occasionally—very occasionally. To be honest I prefer my clubs or the race track. I have a string of horses that have been doing rather well lately. By the way, do you mind if I smoke?"

She shook her head and watched him light a cigar. "Don't you get bored?" she ventured.

"So far not a bit. If you like, I'll introduce you to the London season and I wager you'll find it frivolous but exciting."

Their eyes met and she flushed. "My father is afraid I'll turn into a bluestocking."

He laughed. "There are worse fates than that. Did anyone ever tell you what perfectly marvelous eyes you have?"

She flushed again, this time more deeply. "No," she almost whispered her reply. "I've always considered them far too large for my face."

"Anything but. On the contrary, they're the most honest eyes I've ever seen. One would hesitate a long time before telling you an untruth."

She did not know how to answer him. She had

had no experience in exchanging light banter with a man. He seemed to sense her discomfort and stood up slowly.

"It's getting late," he said. "Let's ride together tomorrow. You'll be served some tea in your room around eight-thirty. Breakfast won't be until much later. So let's meet at the stables. I know just the horse for you, gentle and easy to manage."

She stood up too. "I like them spirited," she replied.

"Then I'll make sure you have a spirited one."

He reached out and took her hand in his. As she looked up at him, he leaned down and brushed his lips gently against hers. "I like you very much, Maria Templeton," he said softly.

"I like you too, but somehow I have a suspicion you prefer blondes." And the picture of him driving along Rotten Row with the beautiful golden-haired woman by his side flashed through her mind.

He laughed. "You're perfectly right. How did you guess? I always have—up until now." Still holding her hand in his, they returned to the drawing room.

The card games were over, the guests enjoying light refreshments before retiring, and as she and the Marquess of Medford entered the room, Maria saw her father and Lord Atherton exchange meaningful glances. She wondered if perhaps the tour of the house with Monty had not been a spontaneous gesture on his part but rather a mission that had been carefully planned in advance.

Momentarily the thought took some of the pleasure out of their encounter, but later as she lay wide awake in the big four-poster bed, watching the moonlight steal into the room, the memory of his brief kiss, the warmth of his hand in hers, crowded every other event of that evening completely out of her mind. For the first time in her short life, she no longer felt an awkward, gauche young girl but a woman—curious and eager for romance.

As she drifted to the edge of sleep, she wondered if Monty kissed every girl he first met and suspected that he did. To him it undoubtedly meant no more than a casual handshake. But to her it had been a momentous event—her first kiss. She hoped he had not realized that. True he had only lightly brushed her lips, but there had been a promise in his eyes as he did so that had left her breathless and a trifle frightened.

The past few days in London she had been annoyed with herself by her inability to erase from her mind their first encounter in Hyde Park. Provoked that she had found herself vainly searching for him every time she rode along Rotten Row, she had lectured herself quite sternly, arguing that, after all, London was an immense city and their chances of meeting again were infinitesimal.

Despite these logical arguments, she had been

unable to forget him and now it seemed almost miraculous that so soon, so unexpectedly, she had met him face to face. A delightful long weekend stretched ahead of them which she knew they would share together. After all, they were the only young people at Longacres and, sighing contentedly, she at last fell asleep.

CHAPTER FOUR

Maria arose early the next morning and was dressed in her riding habit when a servant delivered tea and toast on a metal tray. She smiled at the young maid, neat and demure in her muslin dress, her face scrubbed and shining.

"A beautiful morning for a ride, Miss," she remarked, setting down the tray on a table near the window.

"Yes, isn't it?" Maria moved to the windows and saw that her room overlooked an herb garden and beyond it lay wide green lawns. In the distance stood a collection of gray stone buildings which she guessed must be the stables.

Hurriedly she finished her tea and, leaving her room, encountered no one in the corridors or on the grand staircase. She found the entrance door unlocked and stepped out onto the paved courtyard. An old man was sweeping it with care and bowed to her as she passed by.

It was a wonderful cool May morning and the well-manicured lawns were still wet with dew. She skirted around one wing of the house and found herself in the midst of a formal garden, the hedges neatly trimmed, the flower beds beginning to reveal their first tender buds. Following a brick path, she passed fountains, white statues, and a pond, at last reaching the edge of the lawns that stretched out towards the greenhouses and the stables.

Quickening her pace, finding herself most anxious to ride with Monty, she hoped he had not forgotten the engagement. Perhaps, she thought, in the daylight I won't find him so attractive and the magic of last night will vanish. But even as the idea formed in her mind, she dismissed it as impossible—for deep down she knew this could never be the case.

When she reached the stables, she found him already there, the horses saddled and waiting in the brick enclosure. As he saw her approach Monty called out to her gaily, "Glad you came. I was afraid you might forget."

The horse he had selected for her was a gray mare. As Monty helped her into the saddle, he frowned. "I hope Bess isn't too spirited for you."

She smiled down at him. "No, I don't think so."

She waited for him to mount and then they started off side by side. As he saw how well she handled the mare, he gave a nod of approval and, touching his horse's flank lightly with his heel, he was soon galloping across the green fields with Maria close behind him. They took two hedges with ease and, reaching the woods, cantered along a winding trail.

After a while he slowed his horse to a walk and she drew alongside him. It was cool and peaceful in the woods. Sunlight filtered through the trees and the only sounds were the chirping of birds and the soft plop of the horses' hoofs on the path.

"You ride extremely well," he said.

"Thank you, and I must say you do too."

"You should come for another weekend so we can hunt."

She shook her head. "I don't know if I'd enjoy that. It seems so heartless to have a pack of hounds pursue a frightened fox."

"Well, at least try it once and see. Would you like to rest for a while at my favorite spot?" he asked. Without waiting for an answer, he slipped out of the saddle and helped her to dismount.

They tethered their horses and she followed him into the depths of the woods. She could hear the murmur of a brook in the distance. Clumps of sweet-smelling violets and boulders covered with moss and lichen surrounded them. As they reached a grassy bank, he removed his riding jacket and spread it out for her. The brook was close to over-flowing, the water rushing and swirling past them, running over and around smooth stones and craggy rocks.

"I used to fish here when I was a boy," he re-marked. "This stream abounds with brook trout. And to my way of thinking there is no fish more delectable."

"You should come to New York some day and enjoy the lobster." Maria smiled remembering the well-organized school excursions to the city, where they were marshaled through museums and art galleries and, after the symphony, were allowed to dine at some outstanding restaurant as a special treat.

"I've never been to America, but I've met quite a few Americans girls—debutantes who come over for the season to be presented at court."

"Are we very different from English girls?" she asked.

"A trifle more independent perhaps, but other-wise the same. Actually you're the first woman I've ever met who is quite different. The first one I've encountered who doesn't flirt. I find it most intriguing."

"I'm afraid I don't know how," she confided.

"I can't believe it." His eyes widened in as-tonishment. "I've always understood that girls knew instinctively before they could even walk how to capture the attention of the opposite sex."

"Miss Munson's Academy for Young Ladies gave us little opportunity for that." Maria laughed.

"How long were you there?"

"Six years."

"And your vacations?"

"Lonely ones for the most part—spent on my father's yacht or at our place in the Adirondacks. Sometimes I went to Newport, occasionally Palm Beach. But I have always been isolated. I believe after my mother died my father was really at a loss as to just what to do with me."

"It is high time we remedy that," he said. "Maria Templeton, with your permission it would give me great pleasure to introduce you to the London season. May I be your official escort?"

Their eyes met and Maria felt a thrill of excitement possess her. "You'll find me boring . . ." she began.

"On the contrary . . . ." He moved close to her and she found she was unable to look away from him. It was as if she were completely hypnotized by his warm and ardent glance. His arms stole about her and this time, as his lips met hers, the kiss was not cool and chaste as it had been the night before. As she responded to the pressure of his lips, she shivered and became momentarily lost in his embrace.

"Your second kiss?" he asked, his cheek resting against hers as he stroked her glossy black curls.

"Yes," her voice trembled.

He moved away a little and, with his hands still on her shoulders, studied her. "Moments like this are very rare." He spoke in a low voice and his face had become serious. "And very precious. Don't let's spoil this one by talking."

Gently he took her hand and pulled her to her feet. The black ribbon, which had neatly bound her hair, had fallen to the ground and, reaching for it, he tied it back in place. Without speaking they found their horses and rode back through the woods and across the fields to the stables.

Is this love? Maria wondered, as her horse broke into a gallop. Ahead of her the Marquess of Medford took the first hedge with ease, his red hair shining in the bright morning sunlight. It could be love, she decided, but a little warning bell stirred deep inside her as she remembered Rotten Row and the beautiful blonde who had ridden by his side with such a proprietary air.

Perhaps it's love for me, she decided, but not for him. Maybe this is something he feels he is expected to do and does without thinking—instinctively. Be careful, Maria Templeton, she warned. Along with his gaiety and warmth she had detected something else that she could not pinpoint but found disquieting. Could it have been a lack of sincerity in his manner, as if he were playing a part that he had played many times in the past with other women and would play again many more times in the future?

Impatient with her habit of analyzing people and their motives, she shook off her brief feeling of depression and, when they neared the stables and walked their horses side by side into the courtyard, she accepted the fact that it had been the most glorious ride she had ever experienced. Monty had been correct when he had called it a rare and precious moment.

As all of the guests, with the exception of the Templetons, were accustomed to country house parties, the weekend at Longacres must have held no surprises for them, but to Maria it was an exciting adventure from beginning to end.

Returning from her morning ride with Monty and announcing that she was ravenous, he guided her to the dining room where breakfast had been set up. Large silver dishes warming over spirit lamps contained bacon and eggs, chopped kippers, and even a huge dish of porridge. There were silver pots of tea, coffee, and chocolate, and a cold collation of ham and tongue, pheasant and grouse. As if all that were not enough, she saw a large bowl containing a variety of fruit as well as platters of toast and rolls. They were the last to arrive and found only Sir John Hetherington and her father still at the table.

"I can see now," she said with a laugh, "why so many of you spend part of the year at Homburg or Marienbad."

"Well, you have Saratoga and White Sulphur Springs," Sir John pointed out. "But I have observed, my dear, that you won't have to worry about that for some time to come." He stared with unabashed approval at her slender, young figure in her smart riding habit.

"Are you joining the shooting party, Mr. Templeton?" Monty asked.

"I wouldn't miss it."

"We'll be leaving soon."

"And what do the ladies do while you're gone?" Maria asked.

"Embroider, write letters, read." Monty threw her a mocking glance. "By the way, did you bring your needlework along?"

"No, but I'll read. Your library looks most inviting."

She spent part of the morning curled up on a sofa in the library with a book, exasperated to discover that thoughts of her ride with Monty kept interfering with her concentration. "Don't be a fool," she told herself sternly, when she discovered what she was reading made very little sense. "He's merely being a charming host, and you'd be an idiot to think otherwise."

Despite her admonitions, it was impossible to read and she finally tossed the book aside with an impatient gesture and gave herself up to the luxury of spinning daydreams. He had said he wanted to be her escort during the London season and that meant she would be attending a whirlwind of levees, dinners, and balls with him. She had read enough in the society columns of the newspapers to have a pretty clear picture of what lay ahead. With the King's Coronation, scheduled for June, the season was bound to be even more lively than usual.

Leaving the library, she strolled for a while through the formal gardens, where a staff of gardeners were busily engaged in planting and weeding. She spent some time sitting on a bench by the pond watching the proud white swans glide across the still waters, leaving a path of ripples in their wake.

She lunched with the other ladies in the dining salon. The men had not yet returned from the shoot, and the Duchess of Atherton explained to her that a marquee had been set up in the woods where they were being provided with ample refreshments.

The confusion of so many introductions on the day of her arrival at Longacres had made Maria fearful that she would never be able to memorize all of their names, but she discovered by luncheon time that she now could identify most of the Duchess's guests.

Except for Lady Jane Ashley, they were all middle-aged ladies or older, she noted, and she was pleased when Lady Jane made a point to sit beside her at the table. Maria guessed she was in her late twenties, tall and willowy with ash blond hair and that wonderful creamy complexion that so many Englishwomen are blessed with.

Under cover of the chitchat around them, she leaned close to Maria and whispered, "When this is over would you like to walk to the village? I'm sure the men won't return until time for tea."

"I'd love to," Maria replied eagerly. "After that huge breakfast and this formidable lunch, exercise is what I need."

Luncheon over, she changed into her country tweeds and met her new acquaintance in the entrance hall.

"It's a two-mile hike—are you game?" Lady Jane asked as they waited for a man servant to swing open the heavy oak door.

"I certainly am, but what are the other ladies doing?"

"Either resting or playing cards."

"It's too marvelous a day for that."

They started to walk briskly down the long driveway and Maria breathed in deeply the fresh country air. There was not a cloud in the sky and the massive ancient oaks that lined the road on either side stood proudly, stately, clothed in their tender green leaves.

"Do you live in London?" Maria asked.

"During the season we have an apartment there. But my husband's country home is near Oxford. You must visit us sometime soon."

"I'd love to." Maria smiled happily, delighted to have found a friend. "Which one is your husband?" she asked. "I'm afraid I haven't sorted everyone out yet."

Lady Jane laughed. "That's not surprising—there are so many of us, or so it seems at first. My husband, Charles, is tall, heavy set (though he'd be annoyed at me for saying so), the one with the black hair and very thick beard. He sat across the table from you last night, two down from Monty. Have you placed him?"

"Yes, now I remember him," Maria replied, surprised as she realized that her companion's husband was certainly middle-aged.

"He's lots older than I," Lady Jane explained as if reading Maria's mind. "He's a darling. It's been a very happy marriage. We have a son. My only regret about this weekend is that he had to be left at home. Children are never included in these country house parties. By the way, how was your ride this morning with Monty?"

"Wonderful!" Maria exclaimed, her eyes shining.

"Don't tell me Monty has made yet another conquest." Lady Jane looked amused. "Be wary of him, Maria. Half of the young girls in London are in love with him. He really can't help being a flirt. It is as natural to him as breathing. And then he's so handsome. Don't you agree?"

At her words Maria felt the sparkle go out of the day and was immediately angry at herself for her strong reaction. "Yes, he's very good-looking," she replied quickly and then turned the conversation to the beauty of the day, and how thrilling it was to walk along a country lane between tall hedgerows and green meadows blanketed with sweet-smelling wild flowers.

The village of Eaton, which they had driven through so swiftly the day before, on closer inspection proved to be everything she had imagined an English village should be—with its cobblestoned streets and its gray cottages with thatched roofs clustered closely together on High Street.

Discovering they were thirsty, they found the local inn and ordered tall glasses of lemonade. The proprietor escorted them with great ceremony to a small living room off the lobby and they were grateful to relax in comfortable chairs as they quenched their thirst.

They were rising to leave when the front door opened with a clang and a woman entered. As she brushed past them hurriedly and mounted the stairs to the second floor, Maria caught a brief glimpse of abundant golden curls under a floppy picture hat and eyes that were wide, soft, and gray. She drew in her breath sharply. Surely she had seen the woman before on Rotten Row riding in a gay yellow trap beside the Marquess of Medford.

Out on the street she turned to her companion. "Did you recognize that lady?" she asked.

Lady Jane frowned and gave Maria a puzzled look. "I don't believe so. Why? Did you?"

"I thought I saw her the other morning when I was riding in Hyde Park."

"It's very possible, of course, so many people congregate there. Sorry I can't be of any help though. It was such a brief encounter, but I don't think I've ever seen her before."

They were passing a tiny shop wedged between a bootery and a jewelry store, its windows displaying a lovely array of china. "Come on, let's browse," Lady Jane cried out. "I can never resist browsing and if we don't linger too long, we'll still be in plenty of time to change for tea."

Returning to Longacres, Maria changed into a tea gown before going to the drawing room. The men had rejoined them and were in an exuberant mood, discussing the shoot, which had apparently been successful. As she listened to them comment on the number of birds they had brought down, she was appalled at the enormous quantities of wafer-thin sandwiches, cakes, and cookies that disappeared like magic.

Dinner was scheduled for eight-thirty and after tea everyone retired once more to their rooms for a rest. Maria found Yvette already there filling the metal tub with cans of steaming water. The draperies had been drawn, a fire crackled in the hearth, and the whole atmosphere was warm and relaxing.

"You have a present, Mademoiselle," Yvette said excitedly, pointing to a white box on the table near her bedside.

Maria opened it with trembling fingers to find a delicate corsage of deep red roses nestled in a bed of ferns. An envelope was lying on top and, opening it hurriedly, she read her first note from the Marquess of Medford. In a large careless scrawl he had written—"Thank you for a most memorable ride. Shall we repeat it tomorrow?"

Maria lifted the glistening roses from the box. They were so fresh and fragrant.

"Oh, Mademoiselle, they are beautiful," Yvette cried out. "I caught a glimpse of the Marquess of Medford last night. What a handsome gentleman he is!"

Maria moved toward the fire. "Yes, he is very handsome, and I understand half of the women in London think so too. He's merely being gracious to a rather frightened young girl from America."

She managed to keep her voice steady and casual.

"You underestimate your charm, Mademoiselle," Yvette remarked. "Now, time for your bath and then we must decide what you should wear tonight."

Maria laughed. "Yvette, that's all I've done all day—change clothes. Let me see, first it was my riding habit, next a morning dress, followed by my tweed suit and then this tea gown. Tell me, how did you spend the afternoon?"

"I'm fortunate to be your personal maid," Yvette said. "The housemaids around here do nothing but work. Why, they even carried these cans of hot water to your room. Robert and I really had little to do after lunch, so we took a long walk into the village. There are some interesting little shops there and we had tea in one of them. Now time for your bath and after that a nap. I understand there will be dancing in the gallery tonight and I want you to look your best."

"Yvette, you're spoiling me," Maria protested and realized to her surprise that she thoroughly enjoyed being catered to. If I married Monty, would I sink into this idle life of luxury without a qualm? she asked herself and was shocked to find that her thoughts had carried her so swiftly to the point where even comtemplating marriage to Monty had entered her mind.

At dinner that night Monty was her escort and throughout the lengthy meal she found him an engaging companion as he painted a bright picture of the days ahead. He told her that his mother and father were opening their house on Berkeley Square for the season and were planning a ball. Then there would be the races at Ascot to attend and of course, the most important event of all, the Coronation.

"Will you be part of the ceremony?" Maria asked.

"Oh, yes," he replied with a grimace. "The family state coach has already been taken out of moth balls and is being polished to a fare-thee-well. I'll show it to you tomorrow. It will be transported to London and my parents and I will join the procession to Westminster with a coachman on the box and two footmen accompanying us. We'll be wearing our crimson robes, and I know that I, at least, will feel rather ridiculous.

"It's really highly amusing when you think of it. You see, Queen Victoria ruled for sixty-four years, and as there are only a very few individuals still about who witnessed her coronation, people have been frantically thumbing through historical records and ancient account books for weeks to establish just what the protocol should be. I'll do my best to wangle you a ticket in the stands near the Abbey, so you'll at least see the arrivals and departures."

Later that evening there was dancing. The musicians, gathered at one end of the long gallery, struck up a merry tune with their fiddles. The candles in the chandeliers glowed brightly and the highly polished floor was as smooth as a skating rink.

Maria thanked Miss Munson silently for her insistence on dancing lessons when she joined in a mazurka and later a valse with Monty, as his ancestors looked down at them from their ornate golden frames, in approval or disapproval she could not be certain.

"Doesn't their presence rather overwhelm you?" Maria asked Monty as they paused between dances.

He shrugged his shoulders with indifference. "They've always been there," he answered, "so I rarely think of them. Oh, when I was a small boy I used to study them with curiosity and quite a bit of awe. I've been told that I resemble the fourth Duke of Atherton. Come, I'll introduce you to him." He guided her to a painting in the far corner of the room and she had to agree that he and Monty were very much alike with the same bright red hair and flashing gray eyes.

"I understand he was rather a rake," Lord Montgomery said with a laugh as the musicians tuned up once more. Pulling her to him, they whirled around and around the room.

She found it marvelous to be in his arms and, as far as she was concerned, would have been supremely happy if the musicians had continued playing until dawn, but at twelve o'clock they packed up their instruments and departed while the Athertons' guests made their way to the drawing room for refreshments.

Reluctantly, hand in hand, she and Monty followed them. As they reached the entrance to the drawing room, he said impulsively, "It's far too beautiful a night to stay indoors. Did you know the moon is full? You haven't really seen Longacres until you see it by moonlight. Wait here. I'll return in a moment."

She stood in the doorway watching him move easily among the guests. Her heart was beating rapidly and she was not certain whether this was due to the dancing or because he had asked her to stroll with him in the moonlight.

Surely, she thought, he must like me more than a little to want to prolong the evening. To dance with me was the proper thing to do, only common courtesy, but if he were not at all interested in me, it would have been quite simple to have mingled with the guests in the drawing room instead of suggesting slipping away together.

He was returning now carrying a bottle of champagne and two glasses. "Come," he said and his eyes were sparkling.

She followed him down the grand staircase to the entrance hall and, as he flung open the great doors, they stepped outside.

It was a magical night. The moon silvered the

trees, the wide lawns, the gardens—a perfect setting for romance. They strolled side by side until they found a stone bench near the pond—the bench where she had sat earlier in the day watching the proud swans gliding over the placid waters.

They sipped champagne and he began to speak softly, telling her how much Longacres had meant to him for as far back as he could remember. "I spend a lot of time in London," he said, "but here is where my roots are. Do you find it as beautiful as I do?"

"Yes, it's very beautiful," she said dreamily. "I think without a doubt it is the most romantic place I have ever seen. It is so replete with history. I think of those ancestors of yours in the gallery, encased in their gold frames, and I can visualize them riding through the woods as we did this morning, dancing in the gallery and walking to the village. I don't suppose it's changed very much around here for generations."

"You are exactly right. It has not. And now as the only son, the only heir of Longacres, I find I have a great desire to settle down. Some day this will all be mine and I am becoming increasingly aware that I can't go on much longer living as I do, going to my clubs, to the races, hunting, fishing, rather frittering my life away. I want to change all that—**to** marry."

Maria laughed lightly. "From what Lady Jane Ashley said to me this afternoon, you have a multitude of choices. She told me half the young girls in London are in love with you."

"She exaggerates, but the point is I'm not in love with any one of them. I could never tolerate a marriage of convenience. Could you?"

She shuddered. "No, that would be dreadful. I'm not at all certain how one knows one is in love. I've had no experience, but to marry someone for security or money or some other such reason would be to my way of thinking a grave mistake, and an injustice to the other person."

He slipped his arm about her shoulders and kissed her for the third time. "You are sweet," he whispered and his hand lightly traced the outline of her face—her eyes, her lips, and her strong firm chin. "I find you utterly fascinating. You have no nuances. You are warm and loving and completely honest, a rare combination in this sophisticated society."

They continued to sit there on the bench for some time in silence, savoring the loveliness of the scene around them, reluctant to call an end to the enchantment of the evening. Suddenly the moon was obliterated by a cloud and it grew cold. She shivered.

"It is late," he said. "You must be tired. Shall we ride together again tomorrow?"

"Yes, I'd like that."

They walked back to the great house, kissing

once more, tenderly, gently, before joining the guests in the drawing room.

Soon after she returned to her bedroom, only to discover that the desire to sleep had escaped her. She moved to the windows and saw that the moon again silvered the lawns. She saw a light in the stables—a flickering light. Perhaps one of the stable boys was checking to see that all was well. She undressed slowly, her mind occupied with the events of the weekend, which had changed so completely her narrow, circumscribed world, opening new and fascinating vistas that she had never suspected existed. Before going to bed, she was drawn back to the windows to gaze once more at the moonlight, to relive again the enchanted hour when she and Monty had sat by the pond, drunk champagne, and talked about love.

It was then she heard the sound of horses' hoofs, sharp, unmistakable. Someone was riding along the gravel road that led from the stables to the driveway, and she wondered who it could be at this late hour. Could it be Monty, going to Eaton, to the inn? She had a vivid picture of a woman pushing open the inn door with a clang and brushing past her—a woman with golden hair and wide gray eyes who resembled so strongly the woman in the yellow trap in Hyde Park, who had sat beside Monty, proud and possessive.

Nonsense, she scolded herself. You're imagining

things. She climbed into bed but, tired as she was, it was a long time before she was able to fall asleep. She kept listening for the horse's hoofs on the gravel road, listening in vain for their return.

The next morning they rode again and Monty showed her the state carriage as he had promised. It was very impressive with a huge coat of arms embossed on the panels and silver handles on the doors.

"Possibly this is the last time it will be used." Monty spoke soberly. "Motor cars will soon replace it. Already it's an anachronism, and I'm sure I'll feel foolish riding in it."

Later, after another substantial breakfast, she changed into a violet gown with a short jacket trimmed in sable and walked with Monty and the others to church.

It was another lovely spring day and, as they moved along the country lane, they passed by neat cottages with smoke curling lazily from the chimneys. To Maria it represented a story-book scene. The church bells were pealing in the distance, and as they neared the ancient stone buildings, they were joined by more and more parishioners dressed in their Sunday best, the children scrubbed and shining.

The men and women bowed respectfully to them. Monty seemed to know them all by name and paused here and there to ask questions. Was Mrs. Thayer's rheumatism better now that winter was over? And had the roof on the Webster cottage been satisfactorily repaired? Why, he truly loves this life, Maria thought, despite his occasional scoffing. As they approached the churchyard, she smiled up at him and fervently wished that this lovely holiday could go on forever.

Inside, the church was cool and dim. Little sunlight filtered through the stained-glass windows, and as Maria studied the inscriptions on the walls with interest, she noted that each one was in memory of some member of the Atherton family.

She attempted to concentrate on the sermon, delivered in a quavery voice by the elderly rector, but soon gave up the struggle as her mind wandered back to the dance the night before.

Terribly conscious of Monty's presence next to her in the family pew, she stole a quick glance in his direction, and as she did he smiled his disarming smile which never failed to affect her deeply. Lulled into a mood of enchantment, she sighed contentedly and hoped the sermon would be a lengthy one. The weekend was slipping by far too rapidly. Monday they would be leaving and she was finding it almost unbearable to contemplate bidding Monty good-bye. What if he forgot his promise to look her up in London? What if they should never meet again?

All too soon Monday morning arrived and was spent in a flurry of packing. Valises and trunks were piled high in the vast entrance hall, and the carriages were lined up in the courtyard waiting for their departure.

The Templetons left in the same victoria that had brought them on Friday from the station. Monty helped Maria up the steps, and as the carriage moved forward, he threw her a gay salute and called out, "Remember, I'll see you in London."

"So you enjoyed yourself after all, my dear," her father remarked with an air of great satisfaction.

"Yes, very much." She twisted around to give a final wave to Monty as the carriage started down the long driveway.

"The Marquess of Medford was most attentive," her father added. "And I must say you never looked lovelier."

She frowned. "Father, I was the only other young person there. With no one else for him to be attentive to, he was probably merely being polite."

She caught a twinkle in her father's eyes. "Yes, of course, Maria," he said noncommittally. "I am sure you are absolutely right."

CHAPTER FIVE

When they returned to London, Maria settled easily into the daily routine she had established there—a leisurely breakfast, a ride along Rotten Row later in the morning, a lazy afternoon in the garden with a book, followed by dinner with her father, and an evening game of chess.

By Thursday Maria began to fear that the weekend at Longacres had indeed been a fantasy, a fragile glorious dream that had faded as all dreams do, never to be recalled.

To her dismay, she found herself waiting impatiently for the morning post, her spirits dashed when there was no letter from Monty. It was not until late that Thursday afternoon when red roses arrived for her—a dozen red roses—accompanied by a breezy note that she realized fully the impact he had made on her life. It seemed incredible to her and rather frightening that her moods, her whole outlook, had become so dependent upon what he did or did not do.

The note assured her that he was on his way to London, asking her to save Friday evening for him and, as a matter of fact, every evening thereafter.

Yvette was with her when she lifted the flowers out of their long white box and arranged them in a slender cut-glass vase. Seeing Maria's shining eyes, she smiled with satisfaction as she watched her mistress devour the note and then reread it slowly, not once but several times.

On Friday after her canter in the Park, Maria dressed with great care, selecting a white crepe-de-Chine gown with a wide blue sash, simply but perfectly fashioned. To her the afternoon dragged endlessly. She spent it in the garden attempting with little success to concentrate on a book, impatient with herself that whenever she heard a carriage approaching, she would find her heart beating wildly, hoping it was Monty.

It was late in the afternoon when he arrived. First she heard the loud peal of the front door bell and after a little his voice as he spoke to the butler. As she saw him coming along the garden path, she made an enormous effort to force her eyes to remain on the printed page, to appear nonchalant and cool as if she were accustomed to having countless young men call upon her with great frequency.

He kissed her outstretched hand and then joined her on the stone bench which was set in the shade of a maple tree.

"Thank you for the roses." She spoke with grave formality but when he smiled at her and continued to hold her hand in his, she felt her defenses crumbling. Acknowledging the impossibility of remaining calm and composed in his presence, she was certain that he was fully aware that she had been awaiting eagerly, impatiently, his arrival.

"I've missed you," he said. "Dreadfully . . . I would have come sooner but I had duties to fulfill at Longacres. But now all that is finished and I am free to be with you whenever you wish, and I hope that will be often, Maria."

Her book slipped and landed with a thud on the grass as she became a captive once more to his charms. It was wonderful, yet frightening, to discover that one human being could have such power over her.

She had read about this in books and had considered it rather silly for the heroines to fall completely under the spell of the heroes. She had always labeled them as weak and vapid women and now, to her horror, here she was acting in exactly the same manner, unable to think clearly in his presence, a helpless victim of all sorts of disturbing sensations. Surely it would be impossible for her alone to undergo such a transformation. Surely it took two to strike such a responsive chord.

"I hope you will stay for dinner," she said, reaching for her book and removing her hand from his with a great effort.

"Of course, I was counting on it."

"Father will be delighted to see you."

"And is he the only one who will be delighted?" His eyes had never left her face and she could see that he was highly amused by her formality.

"No," she answered him with a rush of complete honesty. "I will be delighted too."

"That's better," he said with a laugh. "There's no sense in our pretending, Maria, that our meetings are casual encounters. You know as well as I that no matter what the future brings, our lives have been touched and will never be the same again."

"Yes, I feel that too," she replied and was overjoyed to discover that the magic that had existed between them at Longacres was present here in her garden, as strong, if not stronger, than it had been when they sat together in the moonlight, sipping champagne and exchanging tender kisses.

During dinner she was content to sit quietly and listen to her father and Lord Montgomery cover a wide range of topics. She was impressed and sensed that her father too was impressed by

Monty's command of politics and the world of business.

Up until now she was certain her father had classified Monty as a lightweight, a parasite feeding on society, and she glowed with pride that he was also proving a serious side to his nature, that he was able to talk knowledgeably on other subjects besides horses and the gaming tables.

"You should go into business, young man," Samuel Templeton said forcefully and frowned when Monty shrugged his shoulders, as if he considered the business world acceptable to talk about but distasteful to become directly involved in.

"Someday perhaps," he said lightly, "but right now I have other interests." As his eyes found Maria's they held a promise of countless evenings of enchantment.

He departed soon after dinner but not before she had agreed to ride with him the following morning and in the evening to attend a ball.

"You like that young man, don't you?" her father asked when she joined him in the library for a game of chess.

"Yes . . . very much. Don't you, Father?"

Samuel Templeton sighed and lit a cigar with deliberation. "I must admit I was surprised by his conversation tonight," he replied. "Didn't suspect he knew tuppence about business or politics."

"He does sit in the House of Lords, you know," she protested.

"So I have gathered . . . although very infrequently."

As he watched Maria setting up the ivory pieces on the chessboard, he was surprised to discover the depths of his feelings for her. In New York, he had merely considered her a problem to be dealt with as intelligently and efficiently as possible. He had given no thought to the possibility that he would grow to love her dearly. Now he began to doubt whether he had any right to tamper with her life.

Damn it all, he said to himself, that young man is playing his part far too skillfully and it's painfully clear that Maria has been overwhelmed by his tactics.

Samuel Templeton was surprised to realize that he no longer wanted for his daughter what he had so recently schemed and plotted to achieve.

Beginning with the day of Monty's return to London, Maria was swept into a whirlwind courtship that left her breathless and with little time to sort out her thoughts. Soon she lost count of the number of banquets, levees, and balls she attended with Monty always at her side, each one becoming more fascinating than the one before.

If she had paused to ponder, the very suddenness of his attentiveness might have caused her to wonder, to at least open the door to some slight doubts and disturbing questions.

Occasionally she did ask herself why he had selected her from so many others—others who were all too obviously willing and eager to succumb to his charms. But when such a thought did occur, she brushed it aside with impatience, fearful of destroying the delicate fabric of their relationship.

By the second week of June, dignitaries from all over the world, from as far away as Siam and Abyssinia, began to pour into London accompanied by their retinues and vast amounts of luggage. Scarlet stands appeared along the route the royal procession would take to Westminster Abbey and flags of the many nations represented flew from the public buildings. To Maria the colorful scene became a brilliant background to her unexpected love affair.

"I never believed it was possible to be so happy," she told Yvette one evening as she dressed for yet another ball. Monty's attentiveness, his gaiety, his warmth, his charm had made her radiant, adding color to her pale cheeks and depth to her beautiful dark eyes, which up until now had always held a sad and haunted look.

"And why not, Mademoiselle," Yvette replied firmly. "You are young and lovely and are being wooed by the most eligible bachelor in London. Why shouldn't you be happy?"

But Maria shook her head slowly as she watched Yvette brush her luxuriant hair and place a small diamond coronet on her head. "I've seen so many beautiful girls at the balls," she explained, "so much better looking than I that I can't help wondering why Monty selected me. Out of kindness perhaps—a desire to give an outsider a taste of London society?"

"Nonsense!" Yvette slipped a cloak of golden tissue across Maria's shoulders. "You think too much. Enjoy every moment, take what comes your way and don't be so serious, Mademoiselle."

"Yes, I guess I am too serious," Maria admitted. "That's what father keeps telling me." And turning impulsively to Yvette, she gave her a quick hug. "You're my only real friend, Yvette. The English girls I've met here I find very cool and aloof."

"Naturally!" Yvette burst out laughing. "You've stolen the prize."

Maria frowned. "I never thought of it that way. Do you suppose that's why they take great pains to exclude me from their conversations?"

"I'm certain of it. Now go, enjoy yourself to the limit and forget the little cats." And she gave Maria a gentle shove towards the door.

Maria joined in her laughter and hurried downstairs to the drawing room where Monty, splendid in his evening clothes, was waiting for her.

In the second week of June, when the King did not appear for Ascot Week, rumors that his Majesty was ill floated about the town, but the parties and frivolity continued, reaching a fever pitch before it was finally confirmed by five court physicians that the King was to be operated upon immediately for an inflamed appendix.

Maria and Monty were riding their horses in Rotten Row when he told her the sad news.

"What a pity," Maria exclaimed.

"From many points of view," Monty replied, and it was one of the rare times when she had seen a serious expression cross his face. "It's a difficult operation. The King may not recover. And then think of all the expense and waste. The stands will have to be dismantled, and what on earth will happen to all the food that has been ordered? The foreign guests will soon depart. No wonder the King said, 'Will my people ever forgive me?' "

A bright yellow trap drove by and Monty tipped his hat to a stunning lady seated beside her escort. Seeing the woman reminded Maria of the first time she had ridden in Rotten Row when Monty had driven by and given her a gay salute.

"You know," she said slowly, "the first time I met you was here—not at Longacres. It was this exact spot. You were with a gorgeous woman. She was expensively dressed and had the most wonderful golden hair I have ever seen. That's why I said to you once that I suspected you preferred blondes to brunettes."

Monty shook his head, obviously puzzled. "Surely if I had seen you here, I would have remembered. But then I have often ridden along this path with lovely women, so you're probably right. And yes, there was a time when I preferred golden hair to dark—until I met you."

"Will all of this end now that the King is ill?" Maria asked with a sigh.

"If you mean, Maria Templeton, that we will not be together, the answer is no. Isn't it obvious to you that I am falling in love? And that being the case, the important question now is—what do you think of me?"

They were riding side by side and, reaching across, he grasped Sabrina's reins, bringing the horse to a sudden halt. "What do you think of me?" he repeated urgently.

His words forced her to turn and look deep into his eyes. "I think I'm falling in love too." She whispered the words as he leaned towards her and brushed his lips against hers.

It seemed to her eminently correct that their first meeting had taken place here in Hyde Park and that their first confession of love had taken place here also.

He did not propose to her that day but waited until the following evening. It was as if he considered the event so momentous that it must have a perfect setting.

They had attended his parents' ball at their home in Berkeley Square. It was the first time

Maria had seen the Duke and Duchess of Atherton since the house party at Longacres.

The Athertons stood in the entrance hall with Monty beside them greeting their guests, and as Maria shook the Duchess's hand, it was obvious to her that there was no change in their relationship. The Duchess merely bowed her proud head and said a cold good-evening.

But the Duke proved more friendly. As Maria greeted him, he drew her aside for a moment and said, "My dear, today Monty told us of his intentions and I couldn't be happier. I hope your answer to him will be yes." He released her hand slowly.

When she came face to face with Monty, he leaned towards her and whispered, "Don't fill up your dance card, my darling. Tonight is our night and I want you to spend it with no one but me." She moved towards the drawing room, waiting for Monty to leave the receiving line and join her, feeling a trifle lost and lonely among the glittering assembly.

She had to concede the Duchess of Atherton knew how to entertain. It was a beautiful mansion, filled on this warm June night with tubs of spring flowers. The orchestra in the ballroom was already tuning up and the music drifted down the broad marble staircase.

Servants in scarlet livery were circling about

bearing heavy silver trays laden with glasses of champagne. Someone was waving to her across the room and, recognizing Lady Jane Ashley, Maria found her way to her side. Lady Jane was stunning in a silver lamé gown.

"We meet again," Lady Jane said warmly. "I'm so glad. My husband and I arrived two days ago from Oxford and everywhere I've been in London since then you were the main topic of conversation. Is it true, my dear, that you've captured our Monty's heart?" She was sipping a glass of champagne and gave Maria a mischievous grin.

Maria blushed and did not answer.

"Forgive me," Lady Jane said rapidly, "for being so frank. You see, I was about to ask you to visit us when we return to Oxford, but I hesitated when I learned you were already so very occupied."

"Oh, but I'd love to come," Maria answered. "I want to be your friend."

"My dear Maria, you are my friend." Lady Jane hesitated. "And as a friend may I take a small liberty?" With one hand she guided Maria a little away from the others grouped around them.

"Of course."

"You are so young, so vulnerable, Maria. Tread carefully with Lord Montgomery, my dear. I should hate to see you hurt."

"Hurt! How?"

Lady Jane Ashley studied her with a sorrowful expression. "Hurt by Monty, naturally," she finally said in a low voice. "He has been known to hurt people before, unwittingly perhaps, but nevertheless it has happened."

"Lady Jane . . . we love each other." Maria was astounded by her outburst of frankness. "And when two people are truly in love, surely they will avoid hurting each other. It would be inconceivable."

Lady Jane pressed her hand warmly. "If that's the case, Maria, forgive me. I have spoken out of turn and I trust you and Monty will be as happy as my husband Charles and I have been. Forget what I have said and sometime soon visit us in Oxford. Bring Monty too. You'll both always be welcome."

"Thank you, we . . . ." Maria broke off her answer as Monty joined them.

Grasping Maria's hand, he said gaily, "The musicians have begun to play. Come, Maria, remember you promised me the first and every dance."

"Do call on me for tea," Lady Ashley called out after her. "That is, if you can find the time."

The dancing stopped at midnight and the guests were guided towards the dining room to sample a sumptuous buffet.

"I have other plans," Monty said to Maria, holding her back. "Find your cloak, Maria. I'll be waiting for you in the hallway."

A carriage was drawn up at the curb and he

whisked her into it before she could protest. The coachman had apparently already been given his instructions for as soon as they were inside, he cracked his whip smartly and they were on their way.

"Won't your mother consider us rude to leave so abruptly?" Maria asked.

He did not reply. He only smiled and pressed his hand lightly against her lips. "Sshh . . . ," he said softly. "Not a word. We mustn't break the spell."

When they reached Hyde Park, the coachman stopped at the Serpentine. Monty helped her out of the carriage and led her to a bench near the water. The leaves above them rustled, stirred by a sudden breeze. In the daylight, she knew this spot would be a busy place, and the silence around them would be broken by the quacking of the ducks and the chatter of the children as they launched their toy boats under the watchful eyes of their nursemaids.

But tonight they were completely alone with the moon silvering the waters as it had done at Longacres.

"Maria," Monty said without preamble. "Will you marry me?" He sat beside her on the bench, not touching her, waiting for her reply.

There was no question in her mind what her answer would be. Inclined to be a skeptic who up until now had scoffed at story-book romances, who didn't believe in love at first sight, she knew now that she had been wrong, for it was crystal clear to her that she had fallen in love with Monty that first morning on Rotten Row when he had driven by in the yellow trap. How fitting, she thought, that he should propose to me here in Hyde Park where it all began.

"Yes, Monty," she whispered. "I love you and I want to marry you . . . very much."

He gathered her in his arms and kissed her with great passion. Never before had he stirred her so deeply as he did then. They clung together while he kissed her eyes, her cheeks and then once more her lips. She understood at last why men and women have been known to die for love.

"I adore you," he said pulling away a little so he could see her face in the moonlight. "But now, my sweet, I must take you home, for to be honest with you, I don't trust myself in your presence. Tomorrow morning I will call on your father and ask for your hand in marriage. Do you think he will look favorably upon my proposal?"

"He must! If not . . ." She paused.

"If not?" he asked and his eyes were dancing.

"Why, if not, we'll elope."

He laughed an exultant laugh. "My darling Maria, how strange it is that in the last analysis it is I who have become the conservative."

She was too excited to sleep that night and in the morning arose early to catch her father at the breakfast table before he went off to one of his meetings. She asked him to wait with her for Monty's visit.

CHAPTER SIX

Monty arrived at Grosvenor Square at ten o'clock. Maria met him in the hallway and, hand in hand, they went to the library where they found Samuel Templeton working at his desk.

Glancing up, he saw that his daughter's face had acquired a special glow he had never seen before. So it has happened, he thought. Once more he experienced a faint stirring of uneasiness.

During the past few months he had become well acquainted with his daughter and each week had discovered he was more and more impressed by her intelligence, her sensitivity, her innate honesty. He was beginning to wonder if he should confront her with the truth, reveal the plan for a marriage contract. After all, a considerable number of daughters of wealthy Americans had accepted such a situation. Possibly she would accept it too. But as soon as the thought crossed his mind, he dismissed it as completely untenable. He had made a promise to the Duke of Atherton that the agreement would be made in secrecy, and he was not a man to renege on his promises.

In addition, Maria's reaction might be quite the opposite from compliance. He had detected a streak of stubbornness in her character, which she had inherited from him, and he was fearful of the outcome if he, at this late date, laid his cards on the table.

Perhaps he should have allowed her to go to college as she had requested. In March his overriding goal had been to see that she attained a safe and secure niche in society before he died. But now he was beginning to wonder if the world of the British aristocracy would be a happy place for her in the long run. From his observations, he had concluded that it was a shallow and jaded world.

Also at the time he had not considered the possibility that he would become so fond of his daughter, so reluctant to lose her. For lose her he certainly would. When she married Monty, there would be nothing for Samuel Templeton to do but depart for New York and his world of business. Even now he was becoming far too restless and

eager to return to the life he knew and understood.

The Marquess of Medford was speaking, telling him how deeply he loved Maria and asking
with grave formality for her hand in marriage.

Samuel Templeton cleared his throat and stood
up, finding to his amazement that there were
tears in his eyes. Faced with Monty's request, he
knew it was too late to change the course of events,
that there could be no turning back. When he replied, his voice was gruff from the effort to hide
his conflicting emotions. "You are very certain,
Maria, that this is what you want?" he finally
asked.

"Oh, yes, Father." Her voice was breathless, her
eyes shining and, releasing her hand from Monty's,
she moved gracefully across the room to him and
kissed him on the cheek. "I love him, Father," she
said simply.

"But it happened rather suddenly, don't you
think?" he hedged, finding himself deeply moved
by her gesture of affection.

"I love your daughter, Sir," Monty said. "And I
promise you I will give her nothing but adoration and devotion for the rest of her life."

"Yes, yes, I'm sure you will." Samuel Templeton studied the young man standing before him.
Was it possible that the Marquess of Medford,
who apparently had earned the reputation of being a rascal, was genuinely in love with his daugh-

ter? He considered the question for a moment and then dismissed the idea as sheer nonsense. Obviously the boy was a consummate actor, playing the role that had been assigned to him with great dexterity. Having fulfilled his part of the bargain, it was now Samuel Templeton's turn, his obligation, to fulfill his.

It was far too late to turn back the tide. A gentleman's agreement was a gentleman's agreement and, besides, his daughter had been so thoroughly trapped in the web of this romance, it would not only be impossible but heartless to attempt to set her free.

He sighed, managed a feeble smile, and said with false heartiness, "You both have my blessing and now I think we should toast this momentous occasion with a glass of wine." He crossed to a near-by table and poured out three glasses of the golden liquid.

"There will be many details to settle," Monty remarked. "I'm not in favor of long betrothals, Maria, are you?"

But before Maria could reply, her father interrupted. "One step at a time," he said brusquely. "It's more than enough in one day for me to absorb the shock that my only child is betrothed."

Tea the following afternoon at the Duke and Duchess of Atherton's townhouse in Berkeley Square developed into an ordeal for Maria. During her two encounters with the Duke a rapport had been established between them and this continued to be the case. As she entered the formal drawing room, he greeted her with great cordiality, bestowing upon her a fatherly kiss and remarking to Monty what a lucky fellow he was to have won such a prize.

But it was the Duchess who continued to be the problem, treating Maria with the same marked coldness that she had shown to her at Longacres and at her recent ball, convincing the girl by her distant manner that she resented her son's betrothal to an American who bore no title and whose family background appeared obscure to say the least.

Dressed in a flowing gray chiffon gown, the Duchess presided at the tea table with a languorous air. Her remarks to Mr. Templeton and Maria were uttered in a condescending manner.

Is she this way only with us or with everyone, Maria wondered. Glancing nervously at Monty, who was leaning gracefully against the mantel, she was reassured to some extent when he gave her an amused wink.

"We must know your lineage, Mr. Templeton," the Duchess was saying. "For the announcement in the *Times,* you know."

And Maria almost clapped her hands in approval when her father replied with extreme nonchalance. "Merely stating she is the daughter of Mr. Samuel

Templeton of New York, Lake Placid, Newport, and Palm Beach should be quite sufficient."

The Duchess next turned her attention to Maria. "My dear," she said, "I trust you are aware that someday you will become the eleventh Duchess of Atherton. You must not think for one moment it is an easy task. There is far more to it than pouring tea in the drawing room or presiding over a dinner party. Behind the scenes at Longacres are over fifty servants who must be properly managed, and then the people on the estate, of course, they need constant supervision in order. . . ."

"Mother," Monty broke in, "I'm sure you will find Maria a very apt pupil and naturally we all assume and trust that you will hold the title for many years to come. So there is nothing to be concerned about."

Maria was relieved when Monty came to her rescue, throwing him a grateful look, and she was thankful too when the Duke switched the conversation smoothly to another channel.

"You will spend part of the year at Longacres, no doubt," he remarked, "but like all young couples you will need a place of your own in London. We'll have to look into that."

Samuel Templeton cleared his throat and, after asking permission to light his cigar, nodded pleasantly to the Duke. "I've already given it some serious consideration," he said. "I plan to buy property in London. It will be my wedding gift to them. If the Grosvenor Square house is for sale, it would do nicely, don't you think?"

"Very nicely," the Duke of Atherton acknowledged. "Indeed, an extremely handsome gift."

"And the wedding," the Duchess exclaimed. "We must concentrate on the wedding. There will be countless details to iron out. You must be aware, Mr. Templeton, that we are members of the Church of England, ever since the reign of Henry VIII, and it would be inconceivable for an Atherton to be married anywhere but within the Anglican Church. May I ask what is your affiliation?"

"None," he replied easily. "So you see there should be no problem. I imagine Maria will not find it too arduous a task to become a member in good standing of your church. And as for the actual wedding and all the frills and frivolities that accompany it, I, as her father, am prepared to take full charge."

Monty laughed, breaking the tension that permeated the drawing room. "So you see, Mother, it's all very simple. Maria and I will be married . . . it will be done quite properly and you will discover you have not lost a son but, on the contrary, have acquired a very charming daughter."

Samuel Templeton raised his cup to Monty in silent tribute. Maybe he's not quite the bounder I've been led to believe, he was thinking. As he watched his daughter gaze with adoration and pride at her fiancé, his conscience, which had been plaguing him a great deal since the Marquess of Medford's proposal, eased a trifle, for he convinced himself that Maria's great love for her fiancé might very well overcome all obstacles and turn him miraculously from a wastrel into a devoted young husband.

"Don't worry about the Duchess, my dear," Samuel Templeton told his daughter as they returned in their carriage to Grosvenor Square. "I'll be willing to wager that she'll come round, and if she doesn't I don't imagine you and Monty will see too much of her anyway."

Maria was staring out of the window of the carriage, her face troubled. "Monty loves Long-acres," she replied. "You can sense it when you are with him there. Oh, yes, he'll want to go back often to hunt and shoot. Why do you suppose she dislikes me, Father?"

"Because she's a snob and a very selfish woman." Samuel Templeton's face flushed in anger. "We must know your lineage, Mr. Templeton," he mimicked. "What an odious woman!"

Maria burst out laughing. "I was so proud of you," she cried. "You put her in her place very smartly." And then her face clouded over as she recalled the Duchess's comments on the wedding. "I'd be happy to be married quietly with just the family present," she sighed. "But I fear the Duchess of Atherton will make sure it becomes a most elaborate affair."

"In a way it should be."

Maria gave her father a startled glance. "You of all people, Father," she chided him. "I would have gambled almost anything that you would have settled for simplicity."

"Not where my daughter is concerned." He flashed her a warm and tender smile. "I want all of London to admire you on your wedding day. Your mother and I stole away to a justice of the peace. We were poor then . . . poor as church mice. Later I regretted that she could not have been married in the style she deserved, although she never complained. She was a great lady, Maria. Being a Duchess doesn't necessarily make you one, you know."

"I wish mother were alive to be with us now," Maria said wistfully.

Samuel Templeton sighed deeply. "How I wish that too. I find it very lonely without her. I miss her . . . and soon I'll be missing you too. I regret now the many years when I was so involved with business affairs that I neglected you, Maria."

"Oh, Father." Maria grasped his hand impulsively. "Don't have regrets. These past few months with you have made up for everything. Always remember that. I'll miss you too, terribly, but you must visit us often, and of course, we'll come to America. I'm eager for Monty to visit my homeland."

Samuel Templeton squeezed her hand gently and as they rode the rest of the way in companionable silence, he wondered how long it would be before Maria learned that he had very little time left . . . a few months possibly but no more.

The doctor in New York had given him a year and that had been over six months ago. Well, at least when he died, she would not be alone . . . she would have Monty.

He glanced at her surreptitiously. She was looking straight ahead, a smile of happiness on her lips. How much she loves him, he thought, and clenching his big hands together fiercely, he did something he had not done in many years: he prayed. And in his prayer he asked that the Marquess of Medford would always be gentle and kind to his daughter, and that this marriage would change him into a man worthy of her affection.

The illness of the King and the postponement of the Coronation plunged London society into only a temporary period of gloom. When it was announced that his Majesty's operation had been highly successful and his recovery much more rapid than believed possible, the round of festivities increased, if anything, in intensity. Relief was widespread when in July the King convalesced on his yacht in the Solent, setting the date of his Coronation for the ninth of August.

Although Maria would have preferred a small, simple wedding ceremony, it was not to be. For as soon as the announcement of their engagement appeared in *The Times* of London and Monty presented her with a magnificent diamond and sapphire ring, a family heirloom, it became clear that the list of wedding guests would be enormous and that the Duchess of Atherton intended her son's wedding to be one of the most splendid events of the season, surpassed only by the King's Coronation.

As decision after decision was reached without consulting her, Maria was at first annoyed but soon overcame her irritation, determined she would allow nothing to destroy what she knew would be one of the most important occasions in her life.

"Six bridesmaids seems to be overdoing it a little," she remarked to Monty one afternoon as they returned by carriage to Grosvenor Square after a long session with the Duchess. "Particularly since I've met only a few of them and the ones I have met have not been overly cordial to me."

Monty slipped his arm about her shoulders drawing her close to him and, as his lips met hers in an ardent kiss, she reproached herself for the critical note that had crept into her voice. After all, she realized, it wasn't Monty's fault that his parents were prominent personages in England and considered it of the utmost importance that their only son's marriage become a brilliant event.

"The bridesmaids don't matter," he replied soothingly. "Nor my second cousin, Cynthia, who apparently has been assigned the role of your flower girl. . . . Nor seven-year-old Rupert, who will carry the rings on a white cushion, and, forced by his mother to wear velvet breeches, will hate every moment of it."

He was smiling as he stroked her soft dark hair. "Wait until you meet Rupert," he said. "He's the most officious little brat I have ever encountered and I strongly suspect he'll one day become another skeleton in our family closet."

"Do you have many of them?" she asked, amused by his caustic description of another of his seemingly inexhaustible list of relatives.

"Quite a few. . . . My mother, of course, would be shocked to hear me say so and vehemently deny the accusation. Nevertheless, although there have been many Athertons of sterling character, there have also been a goodly number whom we pass over quickly and rarely mention. So when you marry me, darling, you're stuck with us whether you like it or not."

"I'll like it," she replied with a deep sigh of contentment, grateful for Monty's ability to cut through complications with ease and make them seem humorous and rather silly.

"After all," he continued, "the ceremony will last only an hour, the reception not too much longer. It's the honeymoon that's important and I guarantee to you on that occasion there will be only one Atherton present."

"And we'll have the house in Grosvenor Square to return to," she exclaimed. "Now that it belongs to us what fun it will be to redecorate. I plan to toss out all those ugly massive pieces of furniture, rip down the gloomy tasseled draperies and make it spacious and airy."

"I didn't know I was marrying an interior decorator," he said with a laugh. "I take it, as far as you are concerned, the Victorian period is over."

"I'm a novice," she admitted. "I've never bought a table or sofa in my life. You'll have to be patient with the mistakes I'm certain to make."

They had reached Grosvenor Square and as the carriage stopped at the curb, Monty pulled her close to him once more. "I'm busy tonight, Maria," he said. "But perhaps it's just as well you have one evening free without a party. Think about our honeymoon and tomorrow we'll decide where we would like to travel."

"Busy tonight?" she asked, feeling a sharp tug of disappointment. "I thought we'd have a chance after dinner for a few hours, alone, just talking."

"Alone and just talking?" He burst out laughing. "My darling, don't you know that would be impossible?"

The coachman opened the door and she stepped gracefully to the sidewalk. Turning to say good-bye to Monty, she acknowledged his gay salute, and as the carriage jerked and started moving forward, he leaned out the window and called out to her. "Stuffy estate business, Maria. The last night of it, I promise. Sleep well, and we'll go riding in the morning."

She blew him a kiss and remained standing at the entrance to the house, her hand resting on the iron gate until the carriage disappeared around the corner.

"Stuffy estate business," she repeated and it seemed strange to her that he had not mentioned it sooner. All day she had been counting on a few hours alone with him. Now she found herself unable to shake off a sudden mood of depression, for the thought that she would soon be with him alone had helped to control her impatience during the lengthy afternoon session with his mother.

She sighed deeply. The evening would be dreary without him. She opened the iron gate and proceeded slowly up the brick pathway to the house. Without warning, the sparkle had gone out of the day, and although she scolded herself for being too possessive, she was still unable to banish the uneasy feeling that Monty's nonchalant and abrupt departure had not only been most unexpected but somewhat mysterious.

She and her father dined together.

"How was your afternoon with her Grace?" her father asked.

"Tedious."

"I suppose that's the price one pays for marrying into the aristocracy." Her father sampled the wine with an expression of pleasure. "Maria," he said hesitantly, "are you completely sure about this marriage? We can still cancel out, you know. Tongues would wag all over London for a while, but in the last analysis who would really care? We, for example, would be aboard *The Conqueror*, returning to New York, and by the time we reached there, the news would be causing hardly a ripple."

"Father, what are you saying?" Maria exclaimed.

"Forgive me if I spoke out of turn, but I've observed you're very depressed tonight and I thought maybe you were experiencing some regrets."

"No regrets! Lovesick might be a better description. Father, be patient with me for I'm being extremely silly. Monty has a previous engagement . . . some tiresome estate business to take care of. I was disappointed, that's all. I miss him dreadfully and if I don't watch out I will be well on the way to becoming a very self-centered and boring woman."

"That you could never be," her father said forcefully. "And forget my suggestion about returning to New York. You see, I am discovering as August approaches that I'm more and more reluctant to give you up. Selfish of me, but it can't be helped."

She gave her father a worried glance. Lately, she had been so immersed in her own affairs, that she realized she had been neglecting him and studying him now closely she was disturbed to notice that he had aged considerably since coming to England and that his hand as he reached for his glass of wine was slightly unsteady.

"You're all right, Father?" she asked anxiously.

"Perfectly. Nothing that a glass of port and a cigar after dinner won't rectify." He gave her a wry smile. "Now tell me. What did her Grace have to offer this afternoon? How many more names have been added to the wedding party?"

And Maria laughed and told him about the obnoxious Rupert and Monty's confession that one of the noblest families in England was human after all and had a considerable number of skeletons hidden in its closet.

CHAPTER SEVEN

To Maria, the ninth of August, the day of the King's Coronation, was only a prelude to her marriage, which was to take place two days later.

Monty had secured an excellent seat for her in the stands near the entrance to the Abbey, and she was awed and deeply impressed by the magnificence of the procession. People about her identified the various regiments that had been gathered from the farthest corners of the Empire as well as from Europe. There were units from India, the Barbadoes, and Borneo, King Edward's own Russian Regiment of Guards, the Hussars from Austria, and the German Dragoons. Lastly the stately carriages arrived, the emblems of the greatest families of England emblazoned on their doors.

It was an impressive sight to catch glimpses of the peers and peeresses in their scarlet robes and feathers hastening into the Abbey to escape a fine rain that had begun to fall, to listen to the splendid choir singing "Vivat! Vivat Rex Georgius!" and then much later, with the ceremony over, to watch the people pour out of the Abbey, climbing into their coaches and carriages and rolling away.

The Athertons were attending a luncheon at Buckingham Palace, followed by an afternoon reception at Dorchester House, and that night Maria was accompanying Monty to a ball at Londonderry House in Park Lane. With only two days left before the wedding, she was thankful for a free afternoon to rest and dress leisurely for the evening's festivities.

The gown she had selected for the ball was made of emerald satin with the longest train she had ever worn, and to wear over it she had selected an ermine cape that just escaped touching the ground. As Yvette brushed and curled her hair, Maria gave her a detailed description of what she had seen outside the Abbey that morning.

"What a shame it had to rain!" Yvette exclaimed.

"It was only a light drizzle. Were you able to see any of the procession?" Maria knew that her father had given all of the servants the morning off to join the crowds along the route to Westminster Abbey.

Yvette nodded her head as she fastened a string of pearls around her mistress's neck. "Robert and I started off together . . . we were pushed and pulled about but we managed to reach Trafalgar Square to catch a glimpse of the King. My, he is stout but nevertheless he still manages to look regal."

"I haven't met him yet, but Monty says I undoubtedly will after we are married. He's visited Longacres many times and is sure to come again. I would have met him at Ascot if he hadn't been ill. I gather he's as enthusiastic about the races as Monty."

Her eyes met Yvette's in the mirror and she saw with a start of surprise that her little maid had lost her usual exuberance and looked sad and troubled.

"What's wrong, Yvette?" she asked gently.

"It's about Robert, Mademoiselle. Today he asked me to marry him."

"And that makes you sad?"

"No . . . on the contrary it makes me happy. But, you see, Robert and I are worried about the future and what will happen to him when Mr. Templeton leaves." And as her eyes filled with tears she brushed them away impatiently and said, "Forgive me. I have no right to burden you with my troubles."

Maria frowned. "Of course, you have," she said decisively, and then her face cleared as standing up she gave Yvette a hug. "Haven't I been telling you we are friends? Besides I have a wonderful idea. I'll ask Monty first thing tonight if he would like Robert to become his valet, and I'm certain he'll agree. Father has been saying right along that Robert is one of the best valets he has ever employed and that he will miss his services when he returns to America."

She clapped her hands with delight. "Just think, Yvette, it will mean the two of you will accompany us on our honeymoon. It's a deep dark secret, but I'll tell you where we are going after the wedding, if you promise not to say one word to anyone . . . first a cruise on the yacht and then to Paris for a while, and after that Vienna. Why just think, Robert will be able to meet your family and you could be married in Paris if that's what you desire."

Yvette's eyes were shining with excitement. "How wonderful that would be," she exclaimed.

"Two story-book romances," Maria said with a smile. "Monty and I and you and Robert on a double honeymoon."

Yvette placed an ermine cape across Maria's shoulders. "I don't know how to thank you, Mademoiselle . . . you are so good and kind." And as she spoke her eyes misted over again with sudden tears.

"I think it's an omen . . . a good omen," Maria

cried, "that we both fell in love at approximately the same time. Wait up for me tonight, Yvette, and by then I'll have Monty's answer, but you're not to worry for I'm certain he'll say yes."

She and Monty drove to the Coronation Ball in the family coach that the Athertons had brought from Longacres. There were two footmen in the rear and the coachman seated on the high box in front.

"It still smells of camphor," Maria remarked with a giggle and then remembered to ask Monty if he would consider Robert for his valet.

"A good idea," Monty replied. "I'm sure my present one, old Digby, will be relieved as he'd much rather stay on the staff at Longacres. In fact, he told me only the other day that he's a dreadful sailor and was dismayed at the prospect of spending some time on your father's yacht. By the way, is there more to this than you're telling me? You have rather a conspiratorial look."

"You're very observant." Maria flashed him a smile of utter happiness. "It's all very thrilling . . . Yvette, my maid, told me this evening that she and Robert are in love . . . so this way they can travel to Paris with us and you and I will undoubtedly be attending not one wedding but two this month."

Monty squeezed her hand. "You look extremely beautiful tonight," he said softly. "So superbly attired that I've hesitated to kiss you for fear I would destroy the perfection, but I'm going to do it anyway." And smiling tenderly at her, he gently brushed her lips with his. "Each day I discover something special about you, Maria," he murmured huskily. "It's a precious quality you possess to want to create happiness for other people."

They kissed again as the carriage, which had reached Park Lane, lumbered awkwardly to a halt. Londonderry House was ablaze with lights and crowds surrounded the long procession of carriages, murmuring their appreciation as the magnificently gowned ladies descended from their carriages with the aid of liveried footmen.

That night at Londerderry House, Melba sang and afterwards the band struck up a valse. As Maria whirled around the vast ballroom with Monty, she knew that she had reached the very pinnacle of happiness.

Later a buffet supper was served and then the dancing continued. It was close to one o'clock when Maria begged for a reprieve and Monty, after guiding her to a seat in the conservatory, went off in search of some champagne to quench their thirst.

The conservatory was dimly lit and Maria found herself overcome with drowsiness, lulled into a half sleep by the dank odor of luxuriant flowers and plants and the splash of a fountain in the center of the room. She was beginning to wonder what on earth was delaying Monty, when she heard a harsh brittle laugh and a sharp female voice uttering her name. "Do you suppose this Maria Templeton is so completely naive that she does not realize he's marrying her for her fortune?" the woman was saying.

Maria stiffened in her chair, suddenly awake as another female voice floated across the room. "If she doesn't realize it, she's the only one in London not to. Why Estelle was telling me just the other day that she's seen Monty recently with Georgiana on at least three occasions. Rather brazen of him, don't you think? He might have waited until after the wedding."

"Not our Monty!" the other woman replied.

Frozen with horror, Maria sat stiffly in her chair —immobilized, unable to move a finger as in the shadowy conservatory she saw two elegantly clad figures glide from the far corner of the room out into the corridor.

The rest of the evening became a confused jumble for Maria. She remembered Monty returning with the champagne. She remembered being thankful that the room was dimly lit so he could not see her face. She remembered sipping the cool, bubbly liquid, and then saying in a tremulous voice that she was very tired and could they please return to Grosvenor Square. She remembered the rumble of the wheels of the carriage on the cobbled streets and Monty's troubled face as he bent over her.

"You're very pale, darling. Are you certain everything is all right?" he was asking her.

"Yes, of course. I'm only a little tired. I'll be fine by morning."

And all the while she was holding back the tears with a tremendous effort, determined that he would not see her crying. The short drive seemed endless as only one thought dominated her mind —to reach her room at Grosvenor Square where she could find solitude.

But solitude was not to be granted to Maria at once, not until much later. She had bidden a brief good-night to Monty, brushing aside his concern for her lightly. It was not until she had closed the heavy entrance door behind her that she saw a light still burning in the library situated at the far end of the hallway. The murmur of voices rose and fell.

Puzzled that her father was up so late, yet anxious to avoid an encounter, she paused, her foot on the first step of the stairway when she heard the Duke of Atherton's voice say quite clearly, "I apologize for the lateness of the hour, but it was necessary to attend the Prince of Wales's reception."

"No apologizes required." Her father's voice

sounded husky with fatigue. "Although I must admit I grew a trifle uneasy. I want this matter completed before the young people return. It would never do to arouse Maria's suspicions."

The Duke laughed. "Knowing Monty I'd be surprised to see them before sunrise, so I wouldn't worry. But if they should arrive, we can merely say we are two future father-in-laws drinking a toast to their happiness."

There was a pause and then the Duke continued, a solemn note interjected into his voice. "I assume the contract is ready?"

There was a rustling of papers, followed by silence, and Maria moved cautiously across the entrance hall towards the library, so she would not risk missing what was said.

"All in order, my good fellow," the Duke finally broke the silence. "And I might add you've been even more generous than I expected. The annual sum of fifty thousand pounds for Monty is very handsome indeed." He laughed. "Although, no doubt, he'll have no trouble spending it."

Her father sighed deeply.

"Having doubts?" the Duke asked sharply.

"Yes, lately I've been wondering if I have the right to play God."

The Duke's tone when he replied was conciliatory. "Don't worry. Monty will make her happy."

"I wonder." And then her father's mood changed

and in a fairly cheerful voice he suggested a brandy.

Maria stood in the hallway, her hand across her mouth to stifle a scream. Spinning about, she ran rapidly across the thick oriental carpet and up the stairs.

She reached her room breathing hard and flung open the door. In her tormented state at first she did not see Yvette curled up in the chaise longue by the hearth. She was fast asleep. Halfway across the room, Maria saw her and stopped, struggling to control the deep sobs that wracked her body. Wanting at all costs to prevent Yvette from seeing her in such a condition, she tiptoed into the bathroom, plunging her face in cold water and then, glancing in the mirror, ran a comb through her disheveled hair.

Returning to the bedroom, she crossed over to Yvette and tapped her lightly on the shoulder. The little maid stirred and opened her eyes, startled for a moment but relaxing when she recognized her mistress.

"Oh, it's you, Mademoiselle," she said stifling a yawn. And then she sat bolt upright. "Did you speak to his lordship?"

"I did." Maria managed a smile. "And he was very agreeable to the proposition."

"Oh, Mademoiselle, how can I ever thank you?"

"Don't thank me. It's not at all necessary. Just

be happy, you and Robert. And now, as I'm very tired, I must go to bed."

Yvette, remembering her position, scrambled to her feet, blushing. "Mademoiselle, forgive me. Let me help you undress."

"No, Yvette, I'll take care of it myself. It's very late . . . please go to bed."

"You're sure you don't need help?"

"Very sure." Reluctant to have Yvette observe her face, Maria moved to the window and, pulling the draperies back, stared down at the garden below which was still swathed in darkness. Soon it would be dawn and before then she knew she must resolve somehow the earth-shattering problem that had been revealed to her so cruelly, not once but twice this evening.

"Good-night, Yvette," she said wearily and it was not until she heard the bedroom door close softly that she allowed herself the luxury of tears as she threw herself across her big four-poster bed.

Eventually from sheer exhaustion, her sobbing ceased. She rose, undressed, hung her ball gown carefully in the wardrobe and slipped into a silk negligee. Shivering with the cold, as the fire in the hearth had died down long since, she poured herself a glass of sherry and started to pace back and forth across the thick carpeting. Her thoughts moved jerkily from one thing to another. Tomorrow would be her wedding day, the rehearsal at the church was scheduled for this very afternoon, and it was unbelievable to her that only a few short hours ago, as she danced the valse with Monty, she had considered herself, without a doubt, the happiest girl in London.

Now, suddenly, without warning, her happiness had been completely and utterly destroyed. She was consumed by anger—anger at Monty, at the Duke and Duchess of Atherton, and at her father who had, she felt, put her up for sale.

It enraged her to think that they had all stood by, playing their deceitful game, concealing their supercilious smiles as she walked innocently into their trap. She flushed, hot with shame, agonizing over her disgrace.

Her first reaction was to go to her father directly, demand that he cancel the wedding and return with him as soon as possible to America. Surely the contract would be invalid if the ceremony were not performed, and Monty would be left without a bride and her fortune.

That was her first reaction. She would never see the Marquess of Medford or his parents again. She would leave them to their explanations, to cancel the wedding and the reception, and to the unenviable task of facing the gossips in their circle who would be intrigued that their son had been jilted.

The minutes ticked by and it was dawn before she reached her final conclusion, before she rejected the first plan as being the cowardly way out, the easy solution that she would someday undoubtedly regret.

Standing by her window, watching the first faint streaks of light conquer the darkness of the night, she vowed she would marry Monty as she had promised, but with one vast difference—for the wedding vows that she would exchange with him the following morning at precisely eleven o'clock would be made not for love but for revenge.

CHAPTER EIGHT

In retrospect Maria was grateful that so much was crowded into the next two days, leaving her little time to think.

Exhausted, she slept late the morning after the ball at Londonderry House and awoke reluctant to face cold reality. It was one thing to decide alone at dawn what course, what direction, she would give her life, but it was quite another to carry her plan out.

She knew her most difficult task would be to give the impression she was supremely happy, looking forward eagerly to marrying the man of her choice—the man she loved. She allowed herself to be convinced by Yvette that she should have breakfast in bed and as she sipped her tea and played with a piece of toast, she realized that she was actually avoiding for as long as possible the first difficult step—to face her father and appear as if nothing had happened.

Eventually when she did confront him in the library, to her surprise she discovered that it was not as difficult as she had imagined to play her part adeptly.

"Did you enjoy the ball last night?" he asked her.

"Father, Londonderry House was a fairyland. I have never seen more exquisitely attired women or heard a valse played with such perfection. I felt like Cinderella. We didn't dance until dawn but it was close to it before we left." She was ashamed to deceive her father, but nevertheless she was rather proud to learn that she was able to handle the game of deceit so adroitly.

"I'll miss you, Father, dreadfully, when you return to America."

He patted her shoulder awkwardly. "I fear I will be the lonely one," he said gruffly. "But it will give me great comfort to know my daughter is happily married."

She found herself close to tears, touched by his words. During the restless night, she had at first felt great anger against him, rebellious that he had manipulated her life as he would manipulate one of his many corporations, that he had treated her as a child instead of an equal, and that in the last analysis he was largely responsible for her predicament.

But she studied him closely as he sat behind his massive desk and seeing how pale and worn he had become, she was overwhelmed by a combination of love and pity. Recognizing that his motives, in his mind, had been for her best interests, she instantly forgave him. Somehow it was most reassuring to know there was one person in the world who loved her without reservation.

She and her father drove to St. Michael's Church in the early afternoon. She steeled herself for her first meeting with Monty, fearful he would recognize that she now knew he was not in love with her but only involved in a clever plot to rescue him and his family from disaster. They met at the altar and rehearsed together the age-old ritual of the marriage ceremony, and as they stood there side by side, she was stunned that apparently he was completely oblivious to the trauma she had experienced during the past few hours.

He was gay, debonair; he treated her with tenderness, the epitome of the dashing young bachelor who was deeply in love and looking forward eagerly to a life with the woman he had chosen to be his bride.

If he can dissimulate with such expertise, so can I, she told herself sternly and when he gave her an adoring smile, she returned it in full measure.

Hardened by her harsh awakening, she actually enjoyed the dinner party the Duchess of Atherton gave that evening at her townhouse in Berkeley Square. I suppose my father is paying for this, she thought, sipping a glass of sherry in the drawing room, only half listening to the idle chatter of her bridesmaids as she observed the beautiful flower arrangements and sampled the excellent hors d'oeuvres.

Monty was entertaining his best man and ushers at his club, and with a cynical smile she assumed her father was paying for that too. I've grown up overnight, she suddenly realized, and was amused to discover that the Duchess of Atherton no longer had the power to overwhelm her. She now saw her in quite a different light—as she really was, a shallow, vain, and rather pathetic woman.

Her bridesmaids she classified on the whole as silly and innocuous—except for one, a cousin of Monty's, Lady Charlotte Courtney, whom she had never met before. She was from Cornwall and apparently avoided London society as much as possible, only materializing for family weddings, births, and deaths.

Immediately a rapport was established between them, and it was comforting to Maria to know that at last she had discovered another friend in addition to Yvette. During the formal dinner, she and Lady Charlotte had an opportunity to talk about something besides clothes, country week-ends, and balls. When the Duchess of Atherton frowned at the introduction of serious subjects, Maria merely shrugged her shoulders and continued to converse with her new-found friend, savoring to the utmost the opportunity to annoy her future mother-in-law.

The day of her wedding was warm and bright. Under other circumstances she would have considered it a favorable sign, a portent that her life with Monty would have few cloudy skies, but instead she experienced a reverse reaction, wishing heartily for rain, and it seemed to her that even the weather had joined the conspiracy surrounding her.

Her wedding gown, which had been designed by Worth and, up until now, had filled her with delight whenever she looked at it, today left her completely unmoved. In fact, as she submitted to Yvette's careful ministrations and was forced to listen to her exclamations of praise, she fought against completely breaking down and pouring out the truth to her maid who had always been so kind and understanding. Thank goodness for the veil, she thought, at least no one will have a clear view of my face until the end of the ceremony and perhaps by then I will gain control.

As she descended the stairway from her bedroom with Yvette behind her holding the magnificent white satin train, she saw that the servants had gathered in the hallway and were gazing up at her with wonder and admiration. She even managed to smile at them and to laugh with them when her father declared he did not see how in the world they could manage to get her into the carriage without a mishap.

But everything went smoothly and as their coach moved away from Grosvenor Square, she experienced the strange sensation that she was in a dream, that it was not Maria Templeton who was sitting beside her father on the way to her wedding, but some other person she hardly knew.

She had slept very little since the night of the ball and, as she began to feel light and disembodied and wondered if she might faint before the ceremony was over, the pain that had possessed her lessened. If she could concentrate solely on the mechanics of the marriage service, she would survive it with dignity.

The church was already filled to capacity when the Templetons arrived. The bridesmaids in their azure blue chiffon gowns with matching picture hats were assembled in the vestibule, talking in low voices. There was a stir of excitement as she entered on her father's arm. Someone handed her a bouquet of red roses, the organ pealed out the opening bars of the wedding march, and she proceeded down the red-carpeted aisle looking neither right nor left.

She saw the stately bishop in his flowing robes in front of the altar, and Monty, standing straight and tall in the splendid uniform of his regiment. The last note of the organ faded; there was a slight rustle as the guests seated themselves, followed by the clear tones of the bishop as he spoke the ancient phrases of the marriage ceremony.

She noticed that little Rupert in his black velvet breeches had apparently overcome his aversion to being a member of the wedding party and looked positively angelic. One of the bridesmaids was close to tears and she imagined that if she had had the courage to glance at Monty he would be gazing at her with adoration. But not once did she glance in his direction until the end when one of her attendants lifted her veil and she was forced to turn towards him to accept his kiss. She submitted to it—her lips cold and unresponsive.

"Is everything all right, my darling?" he whispered.

And managing a slow smile she answered, "Yes, perfectly."

The organ began the recessional and, as Monty took her arm, the dream-like trance that had surrounded her ever since her departure from Grosvenor Square departed, replaced by the appalling thought that she was now the Marchioness of Medford, married to a man who did not love her, a man whom she now knew to be a spendthrift, and who apparently cared about nothing but gambling, hunting, and the pursuit of beautiful women whose favors he had no difficulty in winning.

She wondered if he were wishing at this very moment that it was Georgiana, not she, who was walking down the aisle beside him—Georgiana, the golden-haired lady who had ridden with him that day along Rotten Row. For Maria was now perfectly certain that she and Georgiana had met—not once but twice before, the second meeting occurring at the inn in Eaton as she sipped a tall glass of lemonade with Lady Ashley and dreamed about her weekend at Longacres with Monty.

Her face grew even more somber when she realized that the night Monty had sat with her in the moonlight and made love to her, he had been thinking all of the time of Georgiana, wondering how long it would be before he could say goodnight to her and ride to the inn to gather Georgiana into his arms.

Vividly, she recalled the sharp clop of a horse's hoofs along the gravel path. Then she had wondered who it might be, out at so late an hour, but now there was no question in her mind that it had been Monty on his way to his lady love, relieved that his tiresome evening with Maria had at last ended.

Her grip on her husband's arm tightened as anger coursed through her body, but when he looked down at her with an expression of concern, she forced herself to smile.

As he helped her into the coach, carefully tucking in her long train, she was appalled to think that she hadn't the slightest notion of how she would handle a situation which had become far too complicated and intricate for a girl still in her teens to solve.

Her father, overriding the Duchess of Atherton's objections, had taken charge of the reception, applying himself with enthusiasm to the smallest detail. It turned out to be a very grand affair with bubbling fountains of champagne, an amazing selection of delectable refreshments and a wedding cake that was the tallest Maria had ever seen. Standing in the receiving line in the drawing room, Maria listened intently to the names of the guests as they were announced and managed a smile and a word or two for each of them.

"You're doing beautifully, darling," Monty murmured and, as a string quartet at the far end of the long drawing room launched into a Strauss valse, she found herself, despite her misgivings, entranced by the gaiety and beauty of the colorful scene.

Monty, strikingly handsome in his uniform, cut the cake with a flourish, numerous toasts were proposed to the bride and groom, and soon the time drew near for her to mount the staircase and toss her bridal bouquet. Stopping at the first landing, she looked down on a sea of laughing faces, aimed her bouquet directly at Lady Charlotte Courtney, and continued on to her bedroom.

Their trunks had been packed the day before and delivered to *The Conqueror* which was anchored at Cowes, so she had no luggage to concern her. Entering her room she found Yvette, already dressed in her traveling costume, awaiting to assist her out of her wedding gown.

"What a beautiful bride you were today," Yvette exclaimed, skillfully working on the myriad of tiny pearl buttons that had to be unfastened. "All your responses were so strong and clear."

"Were they? Funny, I can't remember." Maria walked to the window and stared down at the garden where some of the guests were strolling about enjoying the warmth of the afternoon sun.

"You must hurry Milady," urged Yvette. "Remember we have a train to catch."

"Milady!" Maria's laugh was tinged with bitterness. "That's right. You know, I had almost forgotten that today I acquired a title as well as a husband. The Marchioness of Medford—doesn't that sound grand?"

Yvette gave her a puzzled glance, disturbed by the sarcasm in her mistress's voice. "Now if you'll let me assist you into your suit," she said uneasily and, walking to the bed, she lifted up a delicate rose satin skirt with a matching blouse and jacket and a bonnet of the same color trimmed with white feathers.

Ready to leave, Maria met Monty at the head

of the stairs and hand in hand they descended, laughing as, all along the route from the entrance hall to their waiting carriage, the guests pelted them with rice and flower petals. Maria paused at the curb to give her father a tremulous kiss. "See you next month," she reminded him. "And don't you dare to leave before our return." Brushing a few tears impatiently from her eyes, she added, "It was a wonderful reception. Thank you for it, and I want you to understand that I know everything you have done was meant to be in my best interests."

She whispered the last few sentences, so she would not be overheard by Monty or the many guests who crowded around them. Stretching out a hand, her husband helped her into the carriage and, as it moved forward, she looked back to give her father one final wave. She left behind her a lonely and puzzled man.

It was close to six o'clock by the time they reached the pier where *The Conqueror* was berthed. The harbor was a picturesque sight, alive with naval vessels and pleasure craft of every description. As they boarded ship with Yvette and Robert a few paces behind them, Monty explained that there was so much activity because the King was expected shortly for a naval review at Spithead.

"Poor fellow—one ceremony after the other," Monty remarked. "Aren't we fortunate to have no social engagements for some time to come?"

As she did not reply, he gave her a perplexed look. "You've hardly spoken one word, my darling, since we left Grosvenor Square. Is anything the matter?"

Avoiding an answer, she warmly greeted the Captain who was waiting for them at the head of the gangplank and introduced him to her husband. "We'll depart immediately, milady," he said respectfully. "My instructions have been to cruise southward along the coast of France. I believe the chef has prepared a cold collation for you in the salon."

"Are you hungry, Monty?" she asked airily.

"Starved—and you must be also. It's unfortunate we were too occupied greeting our guests to enjoy that wonderful buffet your father had prepared."

She laughed. "Unless things have changed, there'll be a constant supply of wonderful buffets aboard *The Conqueror*."

She guided him along the deck to the Grand Salon and was amused to see how impressed he was by the size of the ship, the plenitude of liveried servants, and the luxurious appointments.

"As splendid as the *Victoria and Albert*," Monty commented, admiring the Grand Salon which was decorated in scarlet and white.

"More splendid," Maria replied. "But then you're

accustomed to luxury, Monty, so it must be most gratifying for you to know you're assured of it for the rest of your life."

She tossed her bonnet and gloves on a red velvet sofa and stared at him with a defiant air. "I see there's the inevitable champagne. Let's drink a toast to celebrate our marriage."

Caught off guard by the strangeness of her manner, Monty for once seemed unsure of himself, but after a slight pause he said easily, "That's an excellent suggestion."

Maria stood by, watching her husband expertly uncork the bottle of champagne, filling two glasses to the brim.

"May I make the first toast?" Maria asked and without waiting for his reply raised the fragile glass high in the air and said in a loud clear voice, "Let's drink to Georgiana!"

Monty's face became as pale as death and, when he opened his mouth to speak, no words came out.

"And a second toast," she continued relentlessly. "To our marriage contract, but don't you think my dear father was a shade too generous to give you fifty thousand pounds a year to spend on gambling?"

"Maria," he begged, "please let me explain."

But she shook her head firmly and said with a voice as cold as ice-water, "No, my dear Monty, this time there is nothing to explain."

Monty had left his glass untouched. "The agreement was supposed to be a closely guarded secret. Did your father inform you about it?"

"No—I overheard a conversation the night of the ball at Londonderry House. Two delightful ladies, sitting in the conservatory, exchanged a few words about you and me which completely shattered a silly schoolgirl's dreams of love. And then later, when I returned home, your father was in the library with mine signing the contract. They had no idea I had returned. It was all very cut and dried and businesslike."

"If that is the case I should have thought you would have canceled the wedding." His face was flushed and he began to pace back and forth across the salon in great agitation.

"And become the laughing stock of London and New York? No, my dear Monty, I have far too much pride for that. Besides, I decided it might be rather amusing to acquire a title, and later, at your dear mother's demise, become the Duchess of Atherton."

"What kind of a marriage can we have under such circumstances?" he demanded angrily.

She settled herself on one of the crimson sofas, stifling a yawn. "Oh, it won't be too bad," she said lightly. "Better than many marriages, I wager. I'll expect you to escort me to important social events, of course, and to act the part of the faithful husband. But don't worry, there'll still be plenty of time to continue your love affair with this Georgiana woman or anyone else who strikes your fancy. As I understand it, in your circle infidelity does not cause a ripple as long as there's no open scandal, and we'll be most careful to keep the scandal buried out of sight. Rest assured I'll never give you grounds for divorce, and I don't intend to seek my freedom from you."

"I consider the entire situation preposterous," he said earnestly. "Maria, can't you forgive and forget? Surely you weren't naive enough to think that I had never been with another woman before meeting you. And marriage contracts are quite common today. You must be aware of that."

Maria crossed to the ice bucket and poured herself another glass of champagne. "I am aware," she said coldly, "that you have deceived me, along with your father and mine. You pretended you loved me when you didn't. You continued seeing another woman after you had declared your devotion for me. You married me for one reason only —money. Well, now you have your fortune, so I fail to see that you have any reason for complaint."

Abruptly he ceased pacing across the room and, bending over her, placed his hand gently on her chin and raised her face until their eyes met. "But I do love you," he said tenderly and his bright blue eyes which were usually filled with laughter, had become sober and sad. "And it wasn't all a game. At first, yes, but only at first."

She sighed as she shook her head regretfully. "I wish I could believe you but I can't. I trusted you, Monty, and now all of that trust has vanished— destroyed beyond repair. I loved you until I discovered that the man I believed you to be doesn't exist."

"So our marriage has already become a mockery?" he asked.

"Yes, if you consider a marriage in name only a mockery. I'm sure your parents will be upset when the years go by and we don't provide them with an heir. But I can't live with you if that's what you're asking."

She rose from the couch, exhausted by the exchange. "And now I'm going to my cabin to rest and then change for dinner. I sent a note yesterday to the Captain, by special messenger, stating that we would not be sharing the same suite."

"He must have considered it a very strange request," Monty said bitterly.

But she did not answer him as she swiftly collected her bonnet and gloves and left the salon without another glance in his direction.

CHAPTER NINE

Maria soon discovered that it was one thing to take a particular stand and quite another to stick to it. Not that she wavered for one instant in her firm conviction that it was impossible for her to forgive Monty and become his devoted wife. But after a lengthy dinner which they ate in silence in the dining salon, seated at opposite ends of the long table, and after a sleepless night, she accepted the fact that some sort of understanding would have to be reached between them as it would be inconceivable to spend day after day in each other's company in stony silence.

They met the next morning on deck. Monty was at the rail staring out at the distant coastline of France. It was a cold, cloudy day—the sea, gray and storm-tossed, seemed to Maria to suit perfectly her mood. She pulled her sable coat about her and, moving to his side, placed her hands on the rail. Not knowing where to begin, she simply said, "Good-morning."

He kept his eyes fastened intently on the shore. "Good-morning," he replied. "Did you sleep well?"

"Not at all . . . and you?"

"Very badly."

"I did a lot of thinking," she added.

"And you changed your mind?" He turned to her with his old eagerness and miraculously became the gay, debonair Monty who from the start had had the ability to touch a responsive chord deep inside her.

She shook her head sadly. "No, I haven't changed my mind. But we can't go on like this forever, not speaking, completely hostile to each other."

"So what do you suggest?" He lapsed once more into his somber mood, his voice caustic, the expression on his face morose.

She shivered in the cold wind. "Let's walk along the deck. I'm half frozen."

It was rough and as she turned from the rail and stumbled, he steadied her with one hand. "I have been thinking," she continued, "that we'll be thrown together a great deal, especially on this trip. When we return to England, it won't be quite so difficult. I suppose you'll be occupied with your usual pursuits, and I'll have to build some sort of life of my own. But now let's enjoy our travels and not be constant adversaries. When we first met, we found plenty of things to share together. Do you suppose it could be that way again?"

"Possibly, if we try."

"Well, let's try." She spoke urgently. "I can't abide unpleasantness, can you? And let's agree never to discuss the subject of our marriage again. We said all there was to say last night. It will serve no purpose to review it again and again. It would only make our lives unbearable."

She saw the beginning of a smile. "You agree?" she asked eagerly.

"Yes, I agree. What else is there to do? You know, Maria, for the first time since we met, you remind me of your father. I never before suspected that you had such a tidy, analytical mind. Now for a start how would you suggest we occupy ourselves for the balance of the morning? A game of chess perhaps . . . or reading a good book together?"

She glanced at him sharply—not certain whether he was being serious or sardonic. "I like chess," she said warily.

"Then chess it will be." And with a flourish he flung open the door to the Grand Salon and ushered her inside. And although Maria had to admit it was undoubtedly one of the strangest honeymoons in history, at least she considered it to be preferable to continue on their journey as deadly adversaries.

After a few days at sea, they landed at Cherbourg and took the train to Paris, their compartment piled high with luggage. Yvette and Robert had been assigned to another section of the train, leaving them alone only after they were assured everything was in order.

"They are really in love!" Maria said after Yvette and Robert had left. "It's very reassuring."

"Reassuring?" Monty was staring out the window as they rolled through the peaceful French countryside with its low stone cottages, verdant fields, and peacefully grazing cattle.

"Yes, reassuring to know there are people in this world who simply fall in love, with nothing to gain or lose by their relationship, marrying for one reason only—because they want to be together."

He stirred restlessly. "Maria, you are becoming bitter. I don't like that."

"I don't like it either. But I didn't ask to be disillusioned. Events beyond my control made me so."

"Damn those talkative women. Damn the blasted contract," he raged. "Can't you believe I married you because I loved you? We made a pledge at the altar . . . the words we spoke were beautiful, true, honest. Didn't you feel that too?"

"No," she replied coldly. "I was a mechanical toy on our wedding day, merely going through the motions. There was revenge in my heart, I'm sorry to admit it was there. But it was there and it still is."

"What would you have done if you hadn't met me, Maria?"

"You'll laugh but I'll tell you. I would have gone to college if my father had permitted it."

"And have become an old maid, well-educated, too well-educated to be accepted in society. Maybe you would have ended up teaching school to a bunch of young brats who were not particularly interested in what you had to say."

"Maybe . . . but that didn't happen and here we are on our way to Paris. I love Paris, Monty, don't you?"

"Yes, it's a magnificent city."

"Well, let's enjoy it together."

"Do you think Yvette and Robert will get married?" he asked.

"Oh, yes, I believe so. But it will be all very proper, most circumspect. They are both Catholics so there is no problem regarding religion. However, I'm sure there will be certain formalities to go through. First, she will introduce him to her parents and hopefully they will approve."

"Lucky Yvette and Robert," he said with a certain amount of bitterness. "They must think we have a peculiar arrangement."

"If they do, they are far too discreet to reveal their feelings."

They had engaged a suite at the Ritz. To her delight she discovered that Monty was willing to accompany her to the Louvre, to the Sainte-Chapelle, and to Notre Dame.

At the Hotel des Invalides, they looked down from a balcony into the rotunda where the Emperor Napoleon was buried with his brothers.

"My great uncle was killed at Waterloo," Monty said soberly.

"Wars are such a waste," she remarked. "So many innocent lives destroyed as the King of Rome's was. It's a shame Napoleon's son is not buried beside him. Napoleon would have wanted that."

"What a wife he had!" There was scorn in Monty's voice.

"You mean Josephine?"

"No, in her way I believe she loved him. I mean the second wife, the Austrian, Maria Louise. When the going got rough she deserted him and scurried back to Vienna with her child. Well, at least he had a son, although he never saw much of him."

She glanced at him quickly. "Do you want a son, Monty?" she asked.

"Of course . . . very much."

Maria smiled. "Although I can't grant you that, you have a wife who won't desert you."

Monty did not reply as they wandered out into the sunshine, both relieved to be leaving the gloom of Napoleon's burial place behind them.

As Monty had been fascinated by Samuel Templeton's collection of French Impressionists and had spent a great deal of time while they were on the yacht studying them, they spent many mornings exploring galleries and out-of-the-way studios on the Left Bank. To Maria's amazement he spent a portion of his newly acquired income on an exquisite painting of a Degas ballerina.

In addition to sightseeing, they attended the opera, some musical comedies, and light drawing-room plays, and spent lazy hours at sidewalk cafes enjoying an aperitif as they watched the world pass by.

A trip to Versailles and afternoons at the races in the Bois were added to their itinerary with Monty betting on the horses and winning more than he lost.

They allowed Yvette and Robert a considerable amount of freedom, watching the progress of their love affair with keen interest. The day before the wedding Monty again surprised her by presenting the young couple with a handsome purse, telling them it was to be spent for a honeymoon.

"Honeymoon!" Yvette exclaimed. "But Robert and I can't desert you."

They were in the living room of their suite and as she spoke Monty was uncorking a bottle of champagne to celebrate the event.

"Nonsense," Maria exclaimed. "For years at boarding school I managed without a maid and I'm sure Monty will be able to survive for a while without a valet. If not, we'll hire another temporarily. We'll go on to Vienna and you can meet us there."

After Yvette and Robert had gone, leaving them alone in their suite, Maria turned to Monty with a smile. "That was a very thoughtful gesture," she said.

"I'm not an ogre, Maria," he said stiffly. "A fortune hunter, yes, but I do have another side to my nature."

And as he spoke Maria recalled with a rush the days of their courtship before she was aware of the marriage contract—the tender moments, the passionate moments, and particularly the night in the Serpentine when he had asked her to marry him.

Her face softened and she knew that he was right, that there was much about him that was lovable and most endearing. And she wondered if perhaps, in the not too distant future, the bitterness and anger she still felt towards him might diminish and eventually vanish, allowing her to truly become his wife.

A few days before their departure for Vienna,

they attended the simple but lovely wedding in the village of Mantenon.

As Maria sat beside Monty in the church where Yvette had been baptized and later confirmed, listening to the words of the priest uniting the couple in holy matrimony, she struggled to hold back tears and, when Monty covered her hand with his, for the first time she accepted the gesture and did not reject him.

After the ceremony, they attended the bridal luncheon. It was a warm, clear August day. Tables had been set up on the wide lawns surrounding Yvette's parents' cottage and the entire village arrived for the celebration bringing baskets of food and wine. A violinist provided music and Maria and Monty soon became part of the lively scene, joining in the peasant dances, forgetting, if only momentarily, the stark contrast between this and their wedding day.

So the two weeks in Paris, instead of being a nightmare, slipped by rapidly and pleasantly and their last night there, they celebrated with dinner at Maxim's.

To Maria it still was and would always remain a place of enchantment, but this time she felt a part of the people present, rather than a spectator overwhelmed by the setting.

Wearing a white satin gown and the magnificent diamond tiara and necklace which belonged to the Athreton collection and had been presented to her on the day of her marriage, she felt that among all the elegantly clad ladies she was able to hold her own. No longer did she consider herself a shy, slightly gauche little girl. Becoming the Marchioness of Medford had surrounded her with an aura of glamour, and as she tasted the wine and sampled the delicious food placed before her, she was aware that many eyes glanced in their direction and that she and Monty made a very handsome couple.

"My first visit here was with my father," she said to Monty, "and I was overwhelmed."

"You look anything but overwhelmed now," he remarked. "Overnight you have grown up. I remember the first time we met at Longacres, you were so . . ." He broke off looking slightly embarrassed. "But maybe I shouldn't go into that," he finished lamely.

"No, tell me," she urged.

"Well, you were rather like a colt, a bit awkward, slightly unsteady but giving the promise of great beauty as soon as you became adjusted to your surroundings. I was awfully relieved."

"Relieved?"

"Yes, the photograph your father sent to me was not very . . . well not very encouraging."

"My father sent you a photograph?" she exclaimed. "How Victorian—how revolting. It puts me in the category of a piece of merchandise up for sale." She shuddered and the misery of the night when she learned of the marriage contract enveloped her once more, shattering the gaiety of the evening.

Monty, seeing her change of mood, spoke hurriedly. "Remember now, we made a promise not to delve into the past. We've managed pretty well so far, and I must admit, Maria, although it's not the sort of a honeymoon I had been contemplating, I'm really having a good time. Now let's concentrate on how we will spend the balance of our last evening in Paris. Would you consider dancing until dawn?"

That night they did dance until dawn and departed the next morning for Vienna. Monty, who had visited there several times before, took charge, introducing her to a city which for centuries had been the capital of the Hapsburgs—the proud wearers for generations of the crown of the Holy Roman Emperor, until Napoleon had appeared on the stage of Europe and dissolved the Empire.

But the glamour and the traditions were still very much alive in the year 1902, and they enjoyed what they saw immensely—the terraced cafes awash with brilliant flowers, the splendid avenues lined with proud chestnut trees in full bloom, the State Opera House, its ballet dancers unsurpassed anywhere in the world, and the coffee houses where one had to be careful not to order simply coffee, but indicate whether it should be a "cup of gold," "a small brown one," or a *mélange mit Schlag.*"

They drove through the Prater in an open fiacre. They enjoyed a concert in the Stadtpark sipping wine as the musicians in a hatbox bandstand launched into the strains of the *Blue Danube.* They saw the magnificent Lipizzaner stallions at the Spanish Riding School go through a stately quadrille and viewed the daily changing of the guard at the Hofburg Palace, the Emperor's officers splendid in coats of white or blue with scarlet trousers.

Their last night in Vienna they dined in an opulent restaurant and later visited some of the wine taverns they had discovered, lingering at each one, entranced by the music in this city of song.

It was past three o'clock when they returned to their suite at the Hotel Sacher. The slow movement of the open carriage along the moonlit streets, the strains of a violin playing a plaintive Strauss melody, the balmy night air tinged with the odor of flowers, all combined to give Maria a feeling of delicious lassitude, and she made no objection when Monty slipped his arm across her shoulders. Sighing, she even allowed herself the luxury of resting her head against his chest.

"I hate to leave tomorrow," she murmured.

"Why leave then?" he asked. "There's no reason

why we can't extend the honeymoon and possibly make it a real one."

She moved away from him, glad of the darkness so he could not observe her flushed and troubled face. "We've had too much wine," she said unsteadily.

They had reached the entrance of their hotel and Monty helped her out of the carriage. She was wearing a gown of silver cloth with a long train, and as she entered the deserted lobby and watched her husband retrieve their key from the sleepy concierge, her heart was pounding as she realized that her love for him, despite her frequent denials, was an irrefutable fact.

As they took the gilt caged elevator up to their quarters, the wonderful hours they had spent together in Paris and Vienna merged before her eyes into a brilliant kaleidoscope. Surely he must love me too, she thought. Surely his tenderness towards me, his words, his glances contain at least some elements of sincerity. And she began to wonder if she were acting the part of a fool to continue to insist they could never be a man and wife.

In the drawing room, the lights were dim and a decanter of brandy had been placed on a table near the windows. Monty approached it. "A nightcap before retiring?" he asked, giving her a quizzical look as if he were attempting to gauge her mood.

She shook her head slowly. "No, I've had too much wine as it is." And she wondered for an instant if this evening had been part of a plan, to lower her defenses and break through her iron determination never to forget the mockery he had made of their marriage.

"Good-night," she said, managing with a great effort to keep her voice indifferent.

Yvette had left a light burning in her room, the bed neatly turned down, her nightgown and negligee on the chaise longue near the window. She undressed quickly, shivering despite the warmth of the night, and as she tied the cord of her white lace robe about her, she made a sudden decision. She would go to Monty and ask him point-blank if he had fallen in love with her. She must know if his words in the Grand Salon of *The Conqueror*, when he had said, "It wasn't all a game. At first, yes but only at first," had been the truth, and if she had been too wounded, too angry to accept them at face value.

Leaving her room, she moved down the corridor to his and tapped lightly on the door. When he did not answer, she opened it slowly, torn between conflicting desires—the desire to enter and the desire to turn and race back to the solitude and security of her own quarters.

With a mixture of relief and disappointment, she saw he was not there. A single light burned on the desk in the far corner of the room. His bed had been turned down by Robert, his night clothes neatly laid out on the counterpane. Now that she was here, she convinced herself she must remain until they had their confrontation. After all, he was her husband, wasn't he, and she had the right if she wished to be in his bedroom.

Restlessly she wandered towards the desk, thinking perhaps she would switch off the light, that it would be easier to face him in the darkness.

As she raised her hand to plunge the room into blackness, her attention was caught by a thick white piece of paper, lying open on the blotter. Without thinking she lifted it up and saw its contents. It was from London and it was very brief.

My darling, she read, *I miss you dreadfully. The hours without you are endless. Hurry home to your loving Georgiana.*

Dropping the letter as if it were a hot poker, Maria had only one overpowering desire: to escape from the room before Monty entered. Swiftly she opened the door and with immense relief saw the corridor was empty.

Breathing quickly, she reached her room, locking the door behind her. Throwing herself across her bed, she lay there dry-eyed, upbraiding herself for her utter foolishness, for allowing Monty to convince her that he too was finding the days spent with her a marvelous romantic interlude.

Moments later she heard a tap on her door, first light and then urgent. "Maria," he finally called out and, when she gave no reply, he called her name once more before departing.

She did not sleep that night. She lay in her bed staring at the frescoed ceiling, watching the first faint streaks of dawn lighten the room, vowing to herself that never again would she succumb to the well-practiced charms of the debonair but despicable man who had tricked her into this disastrous alliance.

How humiliating it was to discover, at the very moment when she had decided to give herself to her husband, that his liaison with Georgiana had not been broken—that Georgiana had been dominating his thoughts night and day, and that she had been with them everywhere, on the yacht, in Paris, and in Vienna.

How horrifying it was to learn that Monty was capable of such duplicity. And to think that only tonight he had urged her to extend their honeymoon, to make it, as he said "a real one." He had said those words knowing full well that a letter from Georgiana was lying on his desk. Georgiana! How she detested the very name.

CHAPTER TEN

Upon their return to London, Maria threw herself into a frenzy of activity, her first objective being to strip the Grosvenor Square house of its somber draperies, its heavy furnishings, and ornate decorations. It was almost as if by doing so—by discarding the old—that miraculously the dark forebodings which plagued her would be discarded too.

She was both amazed and thankful to discover how many hours of each day she could spend in search of a particular piece of furniture, or deciding what material to select for the draperies or what color scheme should be chosen for the rooms.

Realizing too that Yvette and Robert were entitled to a place of their own, she refurbished an apartment over the stables for them. She and Yvette spent many happy hours selecting fabrics and furnishings.

Long before she completed her task, her father grew restless and laid plans for his departure. She tried in vain to delay his journey, fearful to see the only link with home, with her old way of life, severed.

His last night in London, they dined together and then settled in the library for a talk. It was October, the nights had become chilly, and they were both grateful to share a glowing fire in the hearth.

As Samuel Templeton enjoyed a glass of brandy and an excellent cigar, he studied his daughter with troubled eyes. She had changed dramatically from the frightened girl who had crossed the Atlantic with him last April. She had gained poise and maturity. Always impeccably attired, she could go any place in London society and hold her own without a qualm.

But despite all of this, he was haunted by a vague uneasiness, a suspicion that all was not well with her.

The final remark she had made to him as she started off on her honeymoon with Monty had tormented him ever since, creating the suspicion that somehow, someway, she had discovered the existence of the contract, although how that could be possible remained a puzzle.

Surely Monty would be the last person in the world to reveal the well-guarded secret and the Duke and Duchess of Atherton certainly would not do so. As for him, he was absolutely positive that when he was in the process of drawing it up, he had never left it lying on his desk for one second, always locking it up securely in his safe whenever he left the room.

Fully aware that there were many gossips about, Samuel Templeton wondered if perhaps Maria had overheard some remark regarding her husband's character that had made it clear his courtship had not been spontaneous but contrived.

Several times before his departure he found himself on the brink of asking her point-blank if she was unhappy, if she had any regrets, but each time, when it was on the tip of his tongue to bring the question into the open, he shied away from the confrontation. It was almost as if in the last analysis, he preferred not to know the truth, and so he always wavered and avoided the issue.

The frenzy with which she had tackled the redecoration of her house had disturbed him too. It was as if she were making a giant effort to forget, to immerse herself so deeply in a myriad of details that she would not have time to think.

He had observed Maria and Monty together

countless times in the past few weeks, and to him their manner towards each other had been flawless—polite, pleasant, completely devoid of arguments or disputes.

He frowned as he warmed the brandy snifter in his hands. Perhaps they were too polite and pleasant, he conceded. Perhaps they had established this smooth, unruffled surface to conceal their real relationship.

As for Monty, if he was playing the part of the devoted husband, Templeton had to admit that he was doing it extremely well, without question fulfilling his part of the bargain. As expected, he spent most of each day away from the house—at his club or the races. Some evenings he did not return until late. But he was always on hand for the formal occasions demanding his presence, courtly in his manner towards his wife, presenting the usual gay and light side of his nature to the world.

"Don't look so sad, Father," Maria said, breaking into his thoughts. "Monty and I plan to visit you in America quite soon—certainly by next summer at the latest."

When he did not reply, she asked gently, "What's troubling you? After all you've accomplished your goal; your only daughter is settled and safely married."

"And happily married too," he replied. "That's what I wish to know before I leave."

She struggled to maintain her composure, to sit in the deep chair across from him appearing relaxed and completely at ease. The temptation to break down and reveal her sadness, her disillusionment with Monty, her marriage and her life now and in the future, was great, but somehow she managed to smile blandly and to say easily, "Everything is fine, Father. You mustn't worry about me. What more could a girl ask for than all of this?"

He gave her a sharp, penetrating glance and conceded that he would have to be satisfied with her answer. If she was warning him not to probe or attempt to wear down her defenses, he must respect her warning.

For after all, she was married, the deed was done, and, although he was largely responsible for the course of events, it was far too late to change the decision and turn back.

He sighed deeply, acknowledging that playing God had its disadvantages, creating deep satisfaction at the moment of accomplishment, but leaving the door open for a multitude of regrets and recriminations.

Maria yawned. "I'll write you often, Father, although I suspect you'll find my chatter about the latest ball rather dull reading. Now it's getting late and you start out on a long journey tomorrow." She rose gracefully from her chair and kissed him tenderly on the forehead.

"Good-night, my dear," she said softly, and as she left the room, he knew that he had lost the last opportunity to unearth the unhappiness that he was certain possessed her. He would never again be in a position to beg her to brush aside the past few months, to reject her marriage vows to Monty, and to return home to America with him. For the first time in his life the prospect of tackling the challenges of big business, of out-smarting the tycoons of Wall Street, left him strangely unmoved. At that moment he would have gladly traded his years of success for a closer relationship with his daughter.

It was a gloomy morning towards the end of October. The clouds hung low over the city of London as a cold fine drizzle fell to the ground. Maria was alone in the breakfast room and, as she gazed out the window into the small garden at the rear of the house, she concluded that the drip-ping trees, the tangled flower beds and the soggy piles of brown leaves on the brick pathway ac-curately reflected her mood.

Since her father's departure, when the last link with her former life had been severed, she had experienced more and more frequently long periods of depression. For without her father's presence, she and Monty no longer found it necessary to act the part of a happy, loving couple in front of him, and the result of this lack of any need for prevarication made their situation even more stark and hopeless than it had been at the beginning of their marriage.

With the house completely redecorated and in perfect order, with servants on call to answer her every wish, she felt completely lonely and lost. After all, she thought, staring out at the dreary garden, it was only a partial answer to escape reality in books, and she knew that the time was drawing near when she must plan some direction to her life. But what, she asked herself dispiritedly?

It was at that moment the doorbell was rung with vigor and Lady Charlotte Courtney re-entered her life. Announced by the butler, she strode into the breakfast room in her country tweeds, stated breezily that she had come to town on business and while here was not about to neglect seeing her new and favorite cousin. To Maria, her arrival was like a breath of fresh air blowing through the house.

Somewhere in her thirties, with a rather dumpy figure and a face that could be called pleasant but never pretty, she exuded energy and cheerfulness. As Maria gave her a hug, she remembered with a smile how heartily Lady Charlotte had laughed when she caught the bridal bouquet at the wedding reception.

Now planting a kiss on Maria's cheek, she rejected a cup of tea and began to prowl around the house, inspecting the dramatic changes with avid interest.

"You've worked a miracle, Maria," she exclaimed, pausing to study the Degas painting which Monty had acquired in Paris and which now hung over the mantel in the drawing room.

Maria flushed with pleasure. "But it's all completed. There's nothing more to do." She spoke plaintively.

"And you're weary already of balls and receptions and weekend house parties," Lady Charlotte added with a smile. "I'm not surprised. That's why I chose to live in Cornwall far away from all this folderol. But of course, you have Monty—that makes all the difference." And when Maria did not answer, she threw her a sharp look.

"Disconsolate because the honeymoon is over?" she demanded.

And to Maria's amazement she found herself replying, "Disconsolate because it never really began!" Shocked by disclosing her carefully guarded secret, Maria at the same time experienced a feeling of utter and complete relief.

Lady Charlotte, on the surface at least apparently undismayed by her confession, settled herself into a comfortable chair and said calmly, "I think I'll have that cup of tea after all while you're getting dressed to lunch with me at my club."

Maria shook her head in protest, hoping desperately to avoid revealing the details of her unhappy state to Lady Charlotte. Already she was regretting her sudden, frank outburst and knew a lengthy luncheon would make it impossible to avoid answering her cousin's penetrating questions.

"Nonsense," Lady Charlotte said briskly. "You might as well go and change, for if necessary I intend to sit here all day waiting for you."

Maria was very impressed with the Emerald Club. The walls of the dining room were painted a restful gray and the bright green carpeting was a stunning contrast to the white tablecloths and sparkling cutlery.

"We'll have a sherry first," Lady Charlotte said decisively as she unfolded her napkin. "And after that we'll order our lunch." She gazed about her with an air of satisfaction, bowing slightly to women at other tables whom she recognized. "I'll put you up here as member, if you like."

"That would be most kind of you. I didn't realize that women had their own clubs in London."

"And high time too," her cousin replied. "No reason at all why the men should be the only ones to be exclusive. Not that I have anything against the male sex, you understand, but sometimes it's enjoyable to have a tête-à-tête without any of them hanging around. Now tell me about you and Monty, and there's no sense beating about the bush. If you're having troubles, you're having troubles and the sooner you get them out in the open, the better."

"Whatever I tell you will be kept strictly between you and me?" Maria asked hesitantly, beginning to have more qualms about her unexpected confession to Lady Charlotte.

"Absolutely. You know, Maria, you have to be able to confide in someone, and I'm the old reliable type who wouldn't repeat our conversation to anyone no matter what the circumstances. Tell me, has Monty kicked over the traces so soon? But surely when you married him you must have suspected he was a bit of a bounder!"

Maria's face flushed with embarrassment and misery. "I guess," she said, "I was the only one in London so naive as to believe he was desperately in love with me. Oh, there were a few warning signals along the way, which I chose to ignore. I saw him once in Hyde Park with a beautiful woman but then that was even before I had met him at Longacres.

"And later Lady Ashley made a remark that was disturbing. It wasn't until two nights before our wedding, the night we attended a ball at Londonderry House, that the truth was revealed to me quite brutally, and I was forced to face reality for the first time." She paused, and as she lifted her glass of sherry to her lips her hand trembled. "That is when my lovely dream world was completely shattered," she finished.

"You overheard some old biddies discussing him, I'll wager?"

Maria nodded her head. "And in addition I learned about the marriage contract. I overheard my father and the Duke in the library. That was the final blow. To think I was stupid enough to believe that Monty loved me for myself alone. Can you imagine that up until that night, it never occurred to me he might be more interested in my fortune than me?"

"It was stupid all right," Lady Charlotte said bluntly. "But if you discovered all this before the wedding, why on earth did you marry him?"

"Pride and love for him," Maria replied in a low voice. "I couldn't bear to become the laughing stock of London and New York, and then deep down I hoped that perhaps he really did love me, that it was not merely a game and that on our honeymoon we would reach an understanding.

"Oh, I made it very clear at the outset that I was determined to keep it a marriage of convenience, but by the time we reached Vienna, I was willing to let bygones be bygones. In fact, I was more than willing—I even went to his room the last night there." She concentrated on finishing her glass of sherry, avoiding her cousin's eyes.

"What happened in Vienna?" Lady Charlotte asked.

"Nothing."

Lady Charlotte's eyes were boring into hers relentlessly. "You mean you have never actually allowed him to make love to you?" she asked in amazement.

"Yes, that's what I mean," Maria whispered. "You see, I found a letter from Georgiana on his desk. You can't imagine my despair, my humiliation. Monty, on our wedding trip, had gradually won me over until I was convinced he loved me, so it was a terrible shock to find out at the very moment when I was willing to capitulate that he was still deceiving me. . . . Well, that was the end of all my romantic dreams."

A waiter approached and Lady Charlotte, taking command, ordered for both of them.

"Who is Georgiana?" Maria asked in a tremulous voice. "Do you know her? Has Monty loved her for a long time?"

"I wouldn't classify it as love," Lady Charlotte replied grimly. "She's a Gaiety Girl, one of a long string of Monty's conquests. Georgiana Grey, she calls herself, although I suspect her name is Millie Smith or something equally unglamorous.

"She is blond, gorgeous, and predatory. I suspect before you came on the scene, she believed Monty might marry her eventually despite his family's objections. Apparently she was unaware of the Athertons' tenuous financial position, otherwise she would have dropped him like a hot cake." She chuckled gleefully. "How furious she must have been when your betrothal was announced.

But I suppose she considers that half a loaf is better than none, and she's not adverse to Monty setting her up in a fancy apartment with enough money to buy all the clothes and jewels she wants."

"Do you believe that is what has happened?" Maria asked, fighting back the tears.

"Naturally." Lady Charlotte tackled the fish course with great enthusiasm and then, glancing at her companion and seeing her woeful expression, she put down her fork and grasped Maria's hand which lay limply on the table, squeezed it and flashed her a sympathetic smile.

"After all, Maria . . . what can you expect? I'm not excusing Monty. His treatment of you has been thoroughly abominable, but remember—after marrying him you rejected him completely, and he's not the type of man to remain celibate for very long."

Lady Charlotte beckoned to the waiter and ordered coffee. "Look," she said earnestly, "I know you think I'm being cruel and perhaps I am. But I like you far too well to see you disintegrate into a spineless creature moping about the house. You have too much character for that. Now let's see what your options are. You could divorce Monty, of course. It would create a scandal, but it could be done. On the other hand, if you are too stubborn to give him his freedom, don't act the part of the injured wife which, I must say, does not become you. Why not buck up and turn yourself into one of the most fascinating, sought-after women in London?"

"And how would I accomplish that?"

"It would be a challenge, but it's feasible, for you see, you have the three basic requirements—intelligence, good looks, and an endless supply of money."

Lady Charlotte beckoned to the waiter again and ordered a trifle. "And on second thought I'm willing to help," she continued. "I'll plan to stay at your place in Grosvenor Square for a week or two and, believe me my dear girl, that is a considerable concession. My coachman can return to Cornwall to collect my belongings, and you and I will give a series of dinner parties that will be the talk of the town.

"I know the people to invite—not the light-weights who spend their time discussing who is sleeping with whom, but active worthwhile people. You'd be surprised how many of them we have about. And I'll make a bet with you that before very long you'll find you are the mistress of a salon with a coterie around you that will be the envy of everyone. Why, men and women will be begging for an invitation to one of your dinners or afternoon receptions."

Thoroughly entranced and carried away by her splendid solution and, remembering her history lessons on the French Revolution, she gave a jolly laugh. "Why you'll become the second Madame Roland," she finished with a flourish.

"But she was guillotined in the end," Maria pointed out, laughing too as she found her cousin's boundless enthusiasm contagious.

"But not until she had had a wonderful life," Lady Charlotte pointed out. "Besides, there are no guillotines in England. Well, are you game?"

"Yes, I'm game," Maria replied and, although she was far from certain that her cousin's remedy would be successful, she decided it was only fair to at least give it a try.

On their return trip from Vienna, Maria and Monty had stopped over in Paris long enough to replenish her wardrobe at Worth's and she had had the foresight to engage a French chef, named Raoul, who had trained under Escoffier and was highly recommended.

After dinner that night in Grosvenor Square, Lady Charlotte added her stamp of approval.

"My child," she caroled enthusiastically as they retired to the drawing room, "Raoul is a gem, the icing on your cake. When I think of the fantastic works of art placed before me tonight, I become positively lyrical. What a fool Monty is to miss such a dinner. I suppose he always tells you he is at his club. What a multitude of sins that story usually covers!"

Realizing too late that her last remark, to say the least, was unfortunate, Lady Charlotte hurriedly ordered pen and paper and began to list the names of the guests to be invited to Maria's dinner parties.

Impressed with the names on the list, Maria asked with some trepidation, "But will they come?"

"Of course they'll come," her cousin replied firmly. "On the first occasion it will be out of curiosity, for your marriage, my dear, has stirred up a great deal of speculation—but after that they'll be drawn to your parties like a magnet."

CHAPTER ELEVEN

The following morning was spent busily writing out the formal invitations. The dinner party was scheduled for early the next week.

"Your first party should be small and exclusive," Lady Charlotte explained, paring the original list down to eight individuals.

"Sir John Hetherington," Maria noted with curiosity.

"You met him at Longacres, I imagine."

"Yes." Maria closed her eyes and she was back in the huge drawing room being introduced to Monty for the first time. She had almost forgotten that Sir John was her dinner partner that night, and she smiled as she recalled their spirited discussion of American politics. "He likes Teddy

Roosevelt," she added. "Charlotte, is Sir John a very important individual?"

"Definitely. Recently he's retired from active life, but not too long ago he was a leading power in the House of Commons. Never held a cabinet post, but he was highly respected, the type who works behind the scenes and knows everybody. If he likes you, he'll come out of hiding to support you and that will be half the battle."

"We got along very well at Longacres," Maria remarked. "Monty was amazed. He told me Sir John usually dozed during a lengthy dinner, but instead of that he and I had a very animated conversation. He believed I should go to college. How I wish I had taken his advice."

"No time for regrets," Lady Charlotte warned her sharply. "You'll note I've included Viscount Hartly and his wife. He holds a most important post in the Foreign Office. And also the Earl and Countess of Dahlberry have been asked. They are old family friends, actually they're my godparents. He's one of the leaders in the House of Lords, very erudite and dynamic, and you'll be captivated by the Countess. She's a brilliant conversationalist, always espousing some cause. This year her great interest is the suffragettes. Oh, she doesn't openly support Emmeline Pankhurst's activities, but she's on some sort of committee that gives encouragement to the movement. You might be interested in joining."

The invitations completed, Maria instructed the coachman to deliver them that very afternoon, and she and Lady Charlotte spent the balance of the day with Raoul, planning the menu down to the smallest detail.

That night Maria was surprised when, after dressing for dinner, she entered the drawing room to find Monty there engaged in conversation with his cousin. He was so handsome in his evening clothes that she was unable to avoid a quick upsurge of excitement or to stop her heart from beating faster. Will I never reach the point, she thought with weariness, when he no longer has the power to entrance me?

He was by the fireplace in his favorite stance, one hand resting on the mantel with an air of nonchalance, the other balancing a glass of sherry.

"You didn't tell me Charlotte was staying with us," he said, turning to Maria as she entered.

"As I haven't seen you since yesterday that's not surprising," she replied smoothly.

His face became somber for a moment and he gave her a warning glance as he crossed to a table to pour her a glass of sherry.

"It's all right, Monty," she said. "We don't have to pretend in front of Charlotte. She is fully aware of our predicament."

"Predicament?" Monty gave an amused laugh. "That's a strange way to put it, don't you think?"

Maria accepted the wine. "It's difficult to divine

politely," she replied with a shrug of indifference.

"Here, here," Lady Charlotte intervened. "We are not sparring in the House of Lords, you know. Rather we are looking forward eagerly to one of Raoul's splendid dinners, and, as sparring interferes with the digestive process, I for one will not tolerate it."

"You should have been a school marm, Charlotte," Monty said teasingly.

Nevertheless Lady Charlotte's remark served to clear the atmosphere and they proceeded into the dining room in a fairly affable mood.

"What's this I hear about a dinner party?" Monty asked as the first course was served, "and am I invited?"

"Of course, if you wish to come." Maria found it impossible to keep the frostiness from her voice.

"I certainly do." Maria's heart gave a little leap upward, but he spoiled his acceptance by adding, "Remember, it's part of the agreement. You see, Charlotte, when Maria and I were married, I promised to be a dutiful husband, to be present at all important social functions, but sometimes I feel like a trained seal when I am living up to my part of the bargain."

"You approve of the guest list?" Lady Charlotte asked, refusing to comment on his last words.

"It's smashing," he replied. "And I immediately grasped your intentions. You feel Maria is not fully occupied, that she needs a little stimulation, and I heartily agree with you. As she does not seem to be particularly interested in the promises she made during our wedding, perhaps it is wise that she concentrate on another area, and becoming a hostess might be the answer."

"I warned you my father believed I was in danger of becoming a bluestocking," Maria commented. "And I must admit that the prospect of meeting people who talk of something else beside the latest scandal or who won what at the gaming tables will be most refreshing." She was relieved when Lady Charlotte tactfully channeled the conversation into the subject of Monty's string of horses and how they were performing at the track.

After dinner Monty departed for his club and Lady Charlotte and Maria sat in the drawing room over coffee.

Lady Charlotte smiled at Maria and asked permission to smoke. "A shocking habit," she remarked, settling back with a small cigar and a sigh of deep satisfaction. "You know, Maria," she added as she watched the smoke from her cigar drift towards the ceiling, "I think the groom doth protest too much."

"What do you mean? I'm afraid I don't understand."

"It's quite simple really. If he didn't care for you as you seem to believe, he would treat you with complete indifference. There's an old worn-out saying 'Where there's smoke, there's fire.' Well,

Monty showed a considerable amount of fire to-night. No, Maria, you may think that Monty wants a marriage of convenience as you apparently do, but I don't believe it—not for a minute."

Later that night in bed Maria remembered Lady Charlotte's words and her lips tightened in a thin line. Never, she told herself sternly, never would she take the risk of being hurt and disillusioned by her husband.

To Maria's delight, Lady Charlotte's predictions regarding the effect of her dinner parties proved to be absolutely correct. Quickly they became a success. In fact the word "success" could not possibly describe them. In a relatively short period of time, Maria established herself as one of the leading hostesses in London.

Once assured her protegée was launched, Lady Charlotte Courtney retired with a sigh of relief to her estate in Cornwall, leaving Maria so involved with dinner menus and keeping posted on the latest occurrences in the world around her that she had little time to think about Monty and Georgiana and the debacle of her marriage.

Maria's dinner parties became noted for the superb food and wine and an atmosphere conducive to the free exchange of ideas among her guests. It was not unusual during an evening at the Grosvenor Square house to find the Prime Minister present with his opponent seated directly across from him involved in discussing the Irish

Question or the serious situation in South Africa.

Women's suffrage was a topic that particularly fascinated Maria and although she never became an active member of Mrs. Emmeline Pankhurst's militant group, she did join the more conservative contingent of women who, whenever the opportunity presented itself, spoke in favor of females obtaining the vote.

Without equivocation Maria applauded when the suffragettes invaded the House of Commons, chaining themselves with padlocks to the grilles in the public gallery. Although the members of Parliament were anything but amused by these antics, around Maria's dinner table they had to admit it was quite a sight to see burly policemen carrying out the women and the grilles to some spot where the chains could be severed.

Occasionally Monty joined Maria and her guests and, when he did, his contributions to the often heated discussions were considerable. Listening one evening to his astute summing up of a pressing problem, she recalled that he had done very well at Oxford and felt what a pity it was that he concentrated so much of his energy and talents on gambling and women.

Whenever he sat at the head of the table, presiding over the elaborate meal with an inborn grace, she couldn't help but pretend that they were the happy couple they appeared to be—*en rapport*, compatible, and very much in love.

* * *

As the Christmas holidays approached, Monty
made it clear to Maria that the Duke and Duchess
of Atherton expected them to arrive at Longacres
several days before Christmas and remain there
through the New Year.

As December sped by and the day of their
departure drew near, Maria became more and
more uneasy. It was one thing to share the townhouse with her husband where they had managed
to work out a relatively smooth schedule, each
going his own way with no questions asked, but it
was quite another to become involved in an Atherton house party where she would be at the mercy
of her Grace's sharp tongue and made to feel like
a lonely goldfish, swimming around in a glass bowl,
her every movement under close observation.

"Must we go?" she asked Monty in desperation
the very day before their departure.

"We must," he replied firmly and she was exposed to another side of his nature—Monty, the
traditionalist, who when the chips were down
followed the well-worn path laid out for him by
his ancestors.

As they drove in an open carriage through the
village of Eaton and along the country road to
Longacres, her thoughts drifted back to that weekend in May when she had traveled this same route
with her father by her side, nervous and fearful
of what lay ahead.

But it was winter now and a light powder of snow covered the fields and meadows. The wind was cold and brisk and she pulled the fur rug more closely about her, grateful for its protection.

Glancing at her husband and noting the look of eager anticipation on his face, she grasped for the first time the magnitude of his love for Longacres. As they approached the driveway leading to the great house and she saw in the distance its massive towers and the red and white flag in the courtyard being whipped about in the wind, she had a fleeting hope that at Longacres they might recapture the magic of their first ride together. But it was only a fleeting hope for she knew now, all too well, that while to her it had been magical, to Monty it had been merely the first step in a plot to win not her but her fortune.

Maria had long since become completely exposed to the formalities which were the integral part of a country house party, and she was thankful for the rigid protocol which kept one so occupied changing from one gown to another and consuming vast quantities of food, that there was little desire or opportunity for sustained, intelligent conversation.

She was amused to discover that the Duchess of Atherton was fully informed on her relationship with Monty when she was escorted to her room and found her name only on the printed card on the door and learned that her husband had been assigned to a suite at the farthest end of the long corridor.

As she watched Yvette unpack swiftly and with competence, while a tweeny hauled in the heavy metal cans of hot water, she decided that undoubtedly the most delicate and crucial operation a hostess was called upon to perform was the proper assignment of rooms. By merely strolling down the corridors, one could easily assess who was on intimate terms with whom, and who had been recently jettisoned.

"You won't sit below the salt this time, Yvette," she remarked with a smile and Yvette laughed and said she imagined she might possibly have been promoted to sit on the right of the house steward.

Despite her reluctance to be at Longacres, she was soon caught up in the Christmas festivities, entranced by the beautiful wreaths at the windows, the copper bowls of holly, the ropes of laurel on the mantels and, best of all, the huge evergreen in the great hall, standing in lonely splendor on a dais, glittering with colored baubles, with an angel perched on the topmost branch.

She rode every morning on her favorite mount, Bess, across the fields, through the woods, and past the little brook where she and Monty had exchanged confidences on that day in May which now seemed so long ago. Once dismounting, she wandered to the very spot, her footsteps making a crunching sound on the crusty snow, and stood there for some while watching the black water swirl over and around the frozen rocks and stones.

On Christmas Day she stood beside her mother-in-law in the Great Hall and was touched by the age-old ceremony of the presentation of gifts to the estate children. The candles on the evergreen shimmered as the boys and girls received their presents with shining eyes, while their mothers gathered round the roaring fire holding the babies who were too young to walk.

Later there was plenty of food for everyone, which was consumed with alacrity, and after that Monty approached her and whispered that they were expected to join in the games. Above the noise of the gramophone and the shrill voices of the children, it was with great difficulty they attained order out of chaos and went through the motions of Musical Chairs, Blindman's Buff, and Oranges and Lemons.

Following dinner that night, they attended the Grand Servants' Ball and Maria discovered that protocol here was as rigid downstairs as upstairs. As the wife of the son of the Duke and Duchess, she danced first with the butler and next with the headgroom who guided her expertly through the intricate figures of the Lancers.

Later she whirled around the room with Monty in a valse, waving to Yvette and Robert who were having a wonderful time.

"It's been a lovely day," she said to Monty impulsively.

"I thought you disliked country house parties, he replied.

"I do—usually I find them stultifying, but this somehow is quite different. For how many generations, I wonder, have Athertons attended the servants' Grand Ball in this very room? It gives one an insight into why the British Empire has remained strong."

"So at last you are becoming one of us," he said with a laugh, "although you're obviously still unwilling to provide an heir to continue these great traditions of ours which seem to have impressed you."

"Don't, Monty," she said sharply. "I can't bear to have you talk that way."

The dance ended and turning to Monty, her head held high, she asked him with grave formality if she would be breaking any iron-clad rule if she departed.

He gave her a stiff bow in return and said coldly, "No, we're not expected to linger."

As they left the gaiety and warmth of the Great Hall behind them and returned to the drawing room where a serious game of baccarat was in progress, it took every ounce of courage on her part not to throw herself into his arms, thereby making a complete fool of herself.

* * *

Towards the close of the holiday, she was summoned one morning to the Duchess of Atherton's chambers. Her Grace was still in bed, a pile of letters and household memoranda on her breakfast tray. Maria noticed how exhausted her mother-in-law looked in the bright winter sunlight and was not surprised for she knew that the myriad of details involved in a country house party were overwhelming.

Sitting in a chair near the bed, Maria attempted to begin the interview on a friendly note, although the austere expression on the Duchess's face was ominous.

"We've had a lovely time," she said lightly. "Thank you so much."

The Duchess of Atherton managed a wintry smile and then moved directly to the reasons for requesting Maria's presence.

"I'm considerably disturbed about these dinner parties of yours," she said frigidly. "Trust Charlotte to get you off on the wrong track. I assume she never explained to you that the Athertons do not cultivate people involved in politics, nor do we become friendly with financiers. We consider them several notches beneath us."

"Surely that doesn't apply to the Prime Minister!" Maria exclaimed.

"Well, not the Prime Minister," the Duchess conceded.

"Or Sir Thomas Lipton," Maria added. "Why,

he and the King are very close, I understand."

"That may be," the Duchess sniffed. "But then we do not approve of many of the King's companions. But I'm referring to some of the others you've entertained. In addition, I was appalled to learn that you have become involved in the suffragette movement."

"With the conservative group," Maria protested. "Surely you can't object to my being associated with a committee on which Lady Frances Balfour serves."

"And I understand you actually admire that impossible Mrs. Pankhurst." The Duchess shuddered.

Maria could not suppress a smile. "I don't admire all of her methods, but I do applaud her courage."

"Your function, Maria is not to get involved in the turmoil of politics. Your function is . . . ."

"To produce children," Maria intervened smoothly. "Preferably a son. Well, for your information, I haven't the slightest intention of doing so."

There was a long awkward silence as the two women faced each other, a tremendous gulf between them which seemed to be forever widening.

Finally the Duchess of Atherton sighed deeply and with a sweeping gesture of her hand, signaled to Maria that the interview was over.

"Poor Monty!" the Duchess said mournfully when she was alone once more.

The next day Maria and Monty departed for

London, returning once more to the now familiar pattern of their existence. It was not until February that two events occurred within twenty-four hours that had a tremendous impact on their well-ordered lives.

CHAPTER TWELVE

It was at a dinner party towards the end of February at the Earl of Wallingford's townhouse in Belgrave Square that Maria discovered to her surprise that her husband had been attending the current session of Parliament quite frequently.

The Earl brought the subject to her attention while his guests gathered in the drawing room, chatting and laughing as they were served the best champagne from the Earl's well-stocked cellar.

"Congratulations, Montgomery," the Earl called out as he approached them, and Maria was startled to hear her husband called "Montgomery" instead of "Monty." "I thought your speech today on the budget was smashing. I know it's a rather unpopular stand to take and that it took courage for you to do so, but you're right, you know, absolutely right. We don't share enough of the burden. The handwriting's on the wall, my lad, and sooner or later we'll be forced to comply."

He smiled at Maria. "You should be very proud of your husband," he said. "Must say I was surprised not to see you there in the gallery today applauding him."

Giving Monty a smart slap on the back, the Earl of Wallingford moved on to greet other guests and Maria turned to her husband with a look of astonishment. "I didn't realize . . ." she began, but she did not complete her sentence before Monty interrupted her.

"There's a great deal you don't realize, Maria," he said stiffly, and then added more softly, "there'll be a debate based on my arguments tomorrow. It will be a lively one, no doubt of that. Perhaps you'd care to come and listen."

Accepting his invitation as a challenge, she arrived at the House of Lords early the next afternoon, finding a seat in the packed gallery with some difficulty. The debate was already in progress and she followed it with keen interest.

There was no doubt that Monty's position was being severely attacked and she marveled at his cool replies, unpopular to be sure with the majority of his peers, but so well constructed and delivered, that it was impossible to brush them aside.

She felt a thrill of excitement as she followed the debate and for the first time she accepted the fact that her husband was no longer a dilettante but, on the contrary, was developing into an orator whose words were being seriously considered by both his supporters and the opposition. She wondered if it were merely a passing fancy with him, a temporary diversion and then decided that it was not, that at last Monty had found something to engage his attention besides the frivolities of the social scene.

Finally, in the late afternoon the debate ended and Maria hurriedly left the gallery, eager to return home, hoping fervently that Monty would join her for dinner and looking forward to the opportunity of at last finding a common ground with him.

She was anxious to congratulate him on his part in the dramatic discussion, to tell him how proud she was of him. She was convinced he cared about her reaction, for there was no doubt he had been cognizant of her presence. Several times he had glanced towards the gallery, looking directly at her. Was it conceivable, she wondered, that he was desirous of her support, that he actually cared enough to want his wife's applause? The possibility that this could be true excited her.

Wrapped up in her thoughts, she reached the street not realizing that she had been swept into the midst of a demonstration—a demonstration which had been apparently building up momentum for some time and had reached the stage where it was becoming ugly.

A large group of suffragettes had been vociferously protesting and the police had arrived on the scene trying desperately to establish some sort of order.

She searched anxiously for her coach but was unable to locate it on the busy street. Frightened by the mood of the crowd, she was swept up and carried along with them, unable to escape. Bricks began to fly in her direction. Frantically she ducked, but one hit her squarely on the forehead and with a groan she sank to the pavement, and as blackness descended upon her, she fell into a blessed oblivion.

She awoke much later in her bedroom. Someone she had never seen before was bending over her. He had a kindly face and as her eyes fluttered open he said, "Don't be afraid, Madam. I'm Doctor Richardson. You've had a slight concussion, but you've come out of it and will be as right as rain very shortly."

As he spoke, the shouts and cries of the suffragettes returned to her. She had been hit—yes, she had been hit by something and after that she must have fainted.

"Who brought me home?" she asked.

"Your husband. He was dreadfully concerned and I must inform him immediately that you have regained consciousness." The doctor smiled. "I think he is wearing out the carpet in the library."

He left and she was alone in her bedroom with the fire flickering in the hearth, throwing strange shadows on the walls and the ceiling. She stirred restlessly, wishing her head would stop its steady throbbing.

I had a wonderful dream, she thought. It must have been a dream. I was in our coach and Monty was holding me closely in his arms and murmuring "I love you, I love you, my darling" over and over again.

Terribly tired, she must have drifted off to sleep, for when she awakened Yvette was beside her bed, carrying her breakfast tray. Bright sunshine streamed across the carpet.

"Oh, Milady," Yvette cried. "We are all so glad you are all right. What a terrible fright we had last night. Lord Montgomery was beside himself when he carried you into the house."

Maria pulled herself up on her bed and plumped the pillows behind her. Frightened, she thought, yes he had been frightened, but not for her sake. He was merely afraid that I might die and then what would happen to the marriage contract? Knowing full well how astute her father was in any business transaction, she guessed that he had provided for any contingency, and if she should die there was no doubt in her mind that

Monty's generous allowance and the money that poured into restoring his father's estates would be cut off. Yes, assuredly that was what had upset him so last night.

"Tell him not to worry—that I'm still alive," she said coldly.

Alone once more, she sipped her tea and tried to envision the night before. Wincing, she now had a vivid recollection of the brick flying through the air and her vain attempt to deflect it. And after that? Had it been a dream, her ride in the carriage with Monty pillowing her head tenderly, saying "I love you" or had it actually happened?

Unable to separate fact from fancy, she gave up the struggle and, discovering she was famished, was thankful Yvette had the foresight to bring her a hearty meal.

She had finished her breakfast and was debating whether to attempt climbing out of bed or not when there was a knock on her door and Monty entered. He stood there on the threshold, hesitant, frowning.

"Yvette tells me you're much better," he said. "I'm glad."

She smiled at him tentatively. "Thanks for rescuing me. By the way, I haven't had the opportunity to congratulate you."

"Congratulate me? For what?" He crossed the room and stood gazing out the window at the garden below. He was holding a piece of paper in his hand.

"Monty," she asked sharply. "Is something the matter?"

"Yes. It seems cruel to have to tell you this after what you went through yesterday, but I fear I have no choice. It's your father. . . ."

He turned and stretching out his hand gave her the piece of paper he had been holding. It was a cablegram from her father's sister, Eliza, brief and to the point, stating:

IT IS IMPERATIVE YOU RETURN HOME IMMEDI-
ATELY. YOUR FATHER IS SERIOUSLY ILL AND
WANTS TO SEE YOU.

Her eyes filled with hot tears as she dropped the cablegram on the counterpane and strove to control the sobs that welled up deep inside her.

"You've already read it?" she asked.

"Yes."

"I must go at once, today if possible. Will you book passage for me?"

"Of course, but do you think you're up to it, Maria?"

"Yes, I have to be. You see, he's the only one in this world who cares for me and the only one for whom I care. He needs me and I can only hope I reach his side in time."

"I'll work out all the details." Monty spoke in a

formal, stilted tone. "I'll tell Yvette to pack your belongings." He moved to her bedside and looked down at her with a grave, enigmatic expression. "I'm sorry, Maria, sorry about so many things. But I guess this is no time for soulsearching. Only promise me one thing. You will come back, won't you? You must promise me that you will."

"Of course, Monty," she replied evenly. "I'm not quite certain where my home is anymore, but I guess it's probably, at least for a time, in England."

The trip across the Atlantic was long and arduous. Her father's sister, Eliza, met her at the pier, a tall sparse woman whom Maria had only met a few times and had considered cold and aloof. Today she appeared warm and sympathetic.

"Your father is a remarkable man, Maria," she said. "The doctors are amazed by his grim determination to remain alive until he sees you once more."

"There's no chance for his recovery then?" Maria asked in a low voice.

"None at all, my dear." Eliza reached out and patted her hand. "It's a miracle he is still alive."

The mansion on Fifth Avenue which Maria had always disliked, considering it far too formal and austere, was even more formidable when she arrived on this day in the middle of March. It was sleeting as they drove up to the entrance, the sky gloomy and overcast, and the tall trees surrounding the house were bare and brown, their branches dripping with rain.

Inside it was almost as depressing. A fire had not been lit in the great hallway and the liveried servants tiptoed about the house as if in awesome respect for the man who was about to die. Their faces severe, they seldom spoke and then only in whispers.

She was shocked when she entered her father's bedroom and saw him lying there in the huge walnut bed, a shrunken wreck of a man.

"Father," she said softly.

He opened his eyes with a great effort and, as he lifted his hand from the counterpane, she was dismayed to find how cold it was to the touch, despite the fact that his room was warm, almost hot, with a roaring fire in the hearth.

She pulled a chair to his bedside and sat down, fighting to appear cool and impassive, not to reveal the blow his appearance had dealt her.

"You knew about the contract, didn't you?" he asked. It was so like him to go directly to the point. His voice was so low and quavery she had to bend close to him to catch his words.

"Yes," she replied.

"How did you find out?"

"I came home early the night of the ball at Londonderry House and I heard you and the Duke discussing it in the library."

"Have you forgiven me?" There was a pleading look in his faded eyes.

"Of course, Father," she spoke gently. "I knew all along you believed it was in my best interests. It's not your fault it didn't work out that way."

"You are unhappy with Monty?"

"Yes . . . very. But looking back I'm beginning to realize part of it was my fault. I was hurt, terribly hurt, you see. We never had much chance to bridge the gap between us, and it has been widening and widening ever since."

"Promise me one thing." Samuel Templeton gave a weak laugh. "I've always deplored deathbed promises and here I am asking you to commit yourself to one. I want you to promise me you'll return to Monty and try, try very hard to have a rapprochement. Do your utmost to avoid an open break and possibly a divorce. Divorce is never a very wise solution. Do you think you can give it another attempt? Am I asking too much of you?"

"I'll try, Father . . . I promise you."

"Good." She could see he was completely exhausted, but that her promise to him had made him in some measure happy and at peace, for as she sat there, still holding his hand, he smiled at her and then closing his eyes drifted off to sleep.

She remained by his bedside for a long while before slipping out of his room. That was the last time she saw her father alive, for he died quietly in his sleep sometime in the night.

During the ensuing days, Maria found her Aunt Eliza to be a great help and comfort as they were immersed in a myriad of details—first the funeral, where Maria was touched and almost overwhelmed by the number of people who attended. The church was filled to capacity and until then she had had no comprehension of how many people respected and admired her father.

She had sent Monty a cable at the time of her father's death and one brief letter followed later stating it would be some time before she would be free to return to England.

The months of March and April were spent in long sessions at the lawyers' offices, making decisions, signing papers, and going through the tedious process of settling his estate.

Towards the end of April she felt that her affairs had reached a point where there was no reason why she could not fulfill her promise to her father and return to England, at least temporarily.

Her Aunt Eliza had stayed with her after the funeral and in her own quiet way had offered her advice and support. They had become close friends during the past few weeks.

"I must return to England," Maria told her aunt

one evening as they sat in the huge drawing room of the Fifth Avenue mansion.

Although Maria had not revealed to her aunt the sad state of her marriage, she knew without question that her Aunt Eliza had surmised almost immediately that something was very wrong, and Maria was grateful that she had not probed or asked any questions.

Aunt Eliza smiled. "I'll miss you, my dear. Remember one thing, if ever you need me, I will welcome you to my home in Wallingford." She laughed. "Of course, after London, I am sure it would be quite a letdown, and you would find it anything but glamorous, but it will always be there waiting for you at any time."

"Thank you, Aunt Eliza," Maria said gratefully.

"What do you intend to do about your father's extensive properties and the servants?" Aunt Eliza asked.

Maria sighed. "Nothing for the present. I think it's wrong to make sudden decisions. I've already told the servants to continue on as they have in the past. Later, if I decide to sell the houses and yes, *The Conqueror*, I have promised all of them ample pensions so they will not have to worry."

"You're very generous, Maria," Aunt Eliza remarked.

"There's so much money." Maria raised her

hands in a helpless gesture. "Soon I plan to set up a Foundation in my father's name. The lawyers are already working out the details. There are so many worthy causes, scholarships, endowments. I want his money to be put to good use. So I'll be back, Aunt Eliza, probably in the fall."

The first week in May, she returned to England on *The Conqueror*. It was a tiresome, lonely voyage and she had ample time to think about Monty and her promise to her father. Lying on a deck chair wrapped up in a warm blanket, she puzzled one day over the matter of trying to establish a rapport with her estranged husband, finally deciding that a direct confrontation would be the best approach.

She would simply tell him, when next they met, that she wanted to make a success of their marriage, and that, although she could never completely forget the marriage contract, she was willing to concede that the fault had not been all on one side—that she had been wrong, very wrong, to be so unforgiving, so unrelenting.

She found herself shivering despite the warmth of the spring sunlight, fearful because she was unable to foretell what his answer might be. Surely he'll be willing to meet me halfway, she decided, and as they neared the coast of England, she could hardly contain herself, so impatient she was for the voyage to end. It would be without a doubt a great relief to determine, once and for all, if their future would be spent apart or together.

She had cabled Monty the approximate time of her return. Arriving in Southampton on a cold and rainy day, she boarded the train to London and sat by the window of her compartment, watching the rain streak down the glass. She was a victim of mixed emotions—glad to be on her way to the Grosvenor Square house, glad to be only a few hours away from seeing Monty again, and at the same time fearful of the outcome of their meeting.

Restlessly, she opened *The Times* of London that she had purchased at the station. She had been away from England for such a long time that she felt the need of catching up on the news. Maybe there would be a report of Monty's latest speech in Parliament.

She turned the pages rather listlessly at first until she reached the society section, and there before her eyes was a picture of her husband. He was riding in a smart trap, dressed in morning clothes, a dashing figure with a very attractive woman by his side.

Her hands shaking until the paper rattled, she read the caption. "The Marquess of Medford on his way to the races with Lady Diana Wooding." And below there was a brief account of how well his string of horses had been performing, followed by a sentence that blasted all her hopes for the future and canceled completely her promise to her father. It stated:

> The Marquess of Medford and Lady Diana Wooding have been seen frequently in each other's company these past few months. Recently she became the widow of the late Lord Spencer Wooding.

And so ends my marriage, Maria thought bitterly, and suddenly she became deadly calm, as if she were no longer capable of any emotion. When she reached Grosvenor Square that evening, there were only the servants to greet, and she smiled wearily when she was informed that her husband was "at his club."

Exhausted by the strain of her father's death and this sudden destruction of her hopes for a final chance to end their long estrangement, she went immediately to bed and, before falling asleep, decided that after a few weeks when she was rested and more in control of herself, she would have a talk with Monty, a brief talk, asking for an immediate divorce before she returned to America.

CHAPTER THIRTEEN

As the dramatic meeting with Monty which she had planned so carefully as she crossed the Atlantic never occurred, she settled into the old routine of her London life, pushing aside temporarily the final step in the breakup of her marriage which she now accepted as inevitable.

It was surprising to her how she entered once more with smoothness into the festivities of the London season. She considered it the lull before the final storm. She saw little of Monty at the Grosvenor Sqaure house, but they continued to maintain the formalities, attending the multitude of balls and banquets to which they were invited. Their relationship continued in the now familiar pattern—cool, polite, and completely indifferent.

He had commiserated with her on her father's death in a formal manner, adding that he had been somewhat surprised to receive her cable in which she told him of her plans to return to England.

"I really didn't expect to see you again at all," he had remarked.

And that was the end of any personal exchanges.

Maria went through the motions of the London season like a robot. Half the time she was in a daze, saying and doing the correct things automatically. For the time being the hectic pace protected her like a warm cloak, although she acknowledged that it could not continue this way for very long and that very soon the final confrontation must be faced. She found it to be a peculiar period in her life where she seemed to be marking time, gaining some measure of solace from avoiding the last inevitable step.

To her surprise she discovered she was looking forward to Ascot Week, for with the King fully recovered from his illnesses, it promised to be the most outstanding event of the season. She and Monty were staying at the country home of Lord Billingsly in Berkshire and drove with the other guests to Ascot Heath the morning the races were to begin.

Although she had been told that more often than not it rained during Ascot Week, on this particular day the weather was cooperative and

Maria was thankful, for she had selected for the occasion a flowered voile gown with matching picture hat, which would not have stood up very well in a downpour.

Seated beside her, Monty looked very elegant in his striped trousers, morning coat, and top hat. All along the route to the races the roads were jammed with vehicles and a holiday spirit prevailed among the crowd.

Ascot Heath was prepared for the invasion—its flags flying gaily, its lawns impeccably manicured. In the Royal Enclosure Maria had an excellent view of the procession which opened the festivities. King Edward VII and Queen Alexandra occupied the first carriage, followed by the Prince and Princess of Wales and other members of the royal family.

Between races she strolled about the Royal Enclosure and was busily engaged in conversation with a recent acquaintance of hers, Lady Middleton, when the King approached and asked Lady Middleton to present Maria to him.

"Ah, Lady Maria," he said and she caught a slight twinkle in his eyes. "I've been wanting to meet you. The Prime Minister has mentioned your dinner parties, not once but several times. I think the word he used to describe them was 'stimulating.'"

"I trust they are, your Majesty," she said demurely.

"You have attended Ascot before?"

"Yes, last season, but it was not nearly so exciting without your presence."

His face became somber. "That was a painful period in my life." And then he smiled and his face brightened as he surveyed the gay and laughing people who milled about them.

The King suggested she accompany him to the paddock to watch the horses saddled for the next race, and as they moved along the emerald-green lawns, the crowd made way for them, the gentlemen lifting their hats, the ladies giving deep curtsies.

She studied the horses with great interest.

"Suppose you tell me what horse we should back for the next race?" he asked.

After serious consideration, she selected a coal black horse that caught her fancy. The King told her the horse's name was Blackamoor, his owner the Viscount of Amherst.

"Why did you select him?" he asked curiously.

She laughed and said, "Not for a very good reason, I fear. I like the jockey's colors."

They strolled back together to the enclosure, where she curtsied gracefully and then found her place by her husband's side.

"My, my," he said coldly, "you've created quite a sensation."

She ignored his caustic remark, determined to have nothing spoil her day. Her eyes were sparkling as she watched the horses being led out of the paddock to the track. "The King and I," she said with a mischievous smile, "are betting on Blackamoor." And to her great delight, Blackamoor won in a very close race.

The next day she received a gold cigarette case from the King with a diamond clasp, and when they returned to Grosvenor Square at the end of the week she found a dozen red roses had been delivered that day to the house.

Swept into the mainstream of the London season, Ascot Week faded into the background and it was not until the middle of July, when she was riding her mare one morning in Rotten Row that her brief encounter with the King came once more to the forefront of her mind.

Halfway through her ride, a handsome middle-aged man rode along beside her, tipped his hat gravely, and introduced himself as Sir William Sebastian.

"Have we met before?" she asked curiously, for although his face looked familiar, she was unable to place where and when she had seen him.

"No, but I saw you at Ascot. His Majesty was very pleased when you selected a winning horse for him."

"Oh, you mean Blackamoor," she said with a laugh. "A very lucky choice for I fear my knowledge of racing is extremely limited."

They rode along together in silence for several

more minutes and she was about to say "good-morning" to him and ride away when he leaned close and, speaking rapidly in a low voice said, "His Majesty wishes to have dinner with you tomorrow evening."

Before she could do more than give him a startled glance, he pressed a white card into her gloved hand, tipped his hat again to her, and was gone.

Puzzled, she studied the card. There was only a brief notation on the face of it giving tomorrow's date, the fifteenth of July, and stating that a carriage would arrive for her at precisely eight o'clock. He didn't even wait for my answer, she thought, and then decided that of course he wouldn't. An invitation from his Majesty was undoubtedly not considered an invitation but a command.

She slipped the card in the pocket of her riding habit and, as she rode back to Grosvenor Square, she puzzled over her predicament. At one point she considered seeking out Monty and asking his advice and then rejected the idea as preposterous. By the time she reached the stables in the mews and dismounted, she realized that there was no one in London in whom she could confide.

With a rueful smile, she thought of Lady Charlotte and instinctively knew what her answer would be. She could hear her brisk and hearty voice quite clearly, sweeping aside all obstacles.

"Don't be silly, my girl," she would say. "It's considered a great honor to be a favorite of the King."

Confused and thoroughly agitated, she walked across the mews and into the tiny garden in the back of the house. It was cool there and, as she followed the brick pathway between the rows of neat flower beds, she accepted the fact that it was her problem, hers alone, and between now and the following evening at eight o'clock, it would be up to her to solve it, one way or the other.

It was not until seven o'clock on the evening of the fifteenth of July that Maria made her final decision. She would have dinner with his Majesty. Conceivably his wish was to share a few hours with her with only companionship in mind, for after all he was old enough to be her grandfather. But like everyone else, she had heard numerous rumors of his many affairs, and she was aware that she could not rule out the strong possibility that he fully intended to add her name to the list of glamorous women with whom, over the years, he had established liaisons.

Nevertheless, she told herself firmly, that doesn't mean I have to submit. We will have dinner together, and, if necessary, I will tell him firmly and without equivocation that I will always be a loyal wife. Loyal wife! Her face twisted in a bitter smile. She had never been a wife and since her return to London, it had become all too obvious to her that she undoubtedly never would be. Well, at least, she thought, I will remain true to Monty, and if by doing so I insult the King, it will have to be.

She dressed with great care for her meeting with the King, selecting a red chiffon gown which she had never worn before, considering it a shade too sophisticated. But after all, she decided, she could hardly appear before his Majesty in virginal white. With a defiant air, she instructed Yvette to get out the Atherton diamond tiara and necklace, studying the result with satisfaction in her mirror.

Descending to the drawing room to await the arrival of the carriage, she was startled to find Monty there.

"Not at your club?" she asked, fastening the braided hooks of her red chiffon cape across her throat.

"No, I planned to dine at home tonight, but I see you're going out and are not expecting me to accompany you."

"Hardly," she replied lightly, moving to the great windows that fronted on Grosvenor Square to see if the carriage was approaching.

"I understood it was part of our agreement to escort you to formal dinners and receptions." He spoke stiffly.

"But this is not a formal dinner or reception." Her voice was cool. "Rather, it's an assignation."

She felt Monty's hands gripping her shoulders hard, and as he swung her about she saw that his eyes were blazing with anger.

"What are you talking about?" he demanded.

She drew away from him sharply, lifting her shoulders with a delicate shrug. "Surely you are familiar with the word 'assignation.' You've had so many of them yourself. But this is a very special one . . . it's with the King. You will remember I met him at Ascot and he's been pursuing me ever since."

"You can't be serious! Don't be a fool, Maria!"

"On the contrary, I'm very serious, and I consider myself anything but a fool. Are you thinking your wife is not attractive enough to capture the attention of the King? Or are you fearful perhaps that I will besmirch the Atherton escutcheon and become another skeleton in the family closet?"

Without replying he grabbed her roughly to him, forced her to look deep into his eyes. "Maria," he cried, "don't you realize, don't you have the slightest conception of my love for you . . . my love for you and you alone?"

"What about Georgiana?" she asked with deadly calm, inwardly in turmoil.

"That was over months ago . . . there's been no one since, and if you had allowed me to make love to you that last night in Vienna, I never would have gone back to her."

"Have you forgotten the letter?" Her laugh was brittle.

"What letter? I don't know what you're talking about."

"The letter from Georgiana, of course. I found it in your room that night in Vienna. I can still recall every word of it, and when I read it for the first time, it became crystal clear that you couldn't even accompany me on our honeymoon without continuing your liaison with her."

"She wrote to me . . . not I to her. I had broken off with her long before that."

"And what about Lady Diana Wooding?" she added tauntingly. "Was she Georgiana's replacement or was there a string of other mistresses in between?"

"Lady Diana Wooding," he replied icily, "is my second cousin. I would never contemplate an affair with her. She has been disconsolate since Spencer's death. You were away. Why shouldn't I entertain her?"

"I don't believe you," Maria cried, struggling to break away from his grasp, finding it impossible when, despite her turning and twisting, he forced her down on the sofa. As his lips met hers in a fierce kiss, she closed her eyes, trembling from head to foot, fighting against him but finally becoming lost in his embrace.

Someone nearby nervously cleared his throat. Drawing apart, they saw the butler standing in the doorway, his smooth, impassive face for once betraying uneasiness and embarrassment.

"If you'll forgive me, Milady, the carriage has arrived," he stuttered.

"Thank you, Francis," Maria stood up slowly, adjusting her cape.

"I warn you, Maria, if you go out that door we'll never meet again," Monty stormed.

She did not answer him. She did not give one glance in his direction. When she reached the hallway she saw Francis standing at the open door, waiting for her to pass through. She crossed to the entrance. Outside she could see the opulent carriage, its lamps glowing in the dusk, the footmen at attention waiting to assist her, the coachman in his box ready to snap his whip, and she knew that it was impossible for her to take one step further in its direction.

"Francis," she said softly. "Will you please give the driver a message? Will you say I'm unable to come tonight . . . or any other night."

As she watched the butler scurry down the brick pathway, she touched her bruised lips gently with wonder and delight.

"Monty loves me," she whispered, only now beginning to comprehend the full significance of Monty's angry, desperate declaration. Placing her cape on a chair, she slowly re-entered the drawing room.

Monty was at the window. As she drew near, he heard her approach and turned about.

"Will you mind very much, Monty," she asked tremulously through tears, her face radiant with hope, "will you mind very much to be ostracized from British society? I understand that is what happens when one refuses the King."

And then she was in his arms—as she should have been long ago.

 **Bestsellers**